TIME AMONG THE DEAD

Also by Thomas Rayfiel

Thomas Rayfiel

THE PERMANENT PRESS
SAG HARBOR, NY 11963

For information, address:
The Permanent Press
4170 Noyac Road
Sag Harbor, NY 11963
www.thepermanentpress.com

Library of Congress Cataloging-in-Publication Data

Rayfiel, Thomas–
    Time among the dead / Thomas Rayfiel.
        p. cm.
    ISBN 978-1-57962-201-5 (alk. paper)
        1. Diaries—Authorship—Fiction. 2. Older men—
    Fiction. 3. Aristocracy (Social class)—England—Fiction.
    4. Reminiscing in old age—Fiction. 5. Country life—
    England—Fiction. I. Title.

PS3568.A9257T56 2010
813'.54—dc22   2010003243

Printed in the United States of America.

for Leo and Celia

March 18

Morocco-bound, gilt-edged, with a ribbon to mark one's place, a journal reeks of obligation, which is, I am sure, precisely what Seabold intended, that I should wile away the precious time left me distilling whatever "wisdom" six-and-eighty summers have supposedly deposited in my brain. Faugh! I say to that. I would rather muck out the servants' privy than try extracting from the private nature of my life any such lessons as could be useful to posterity.

Nevertheless, I must pretend to write *something*, as he is here in the room, overseeing the production of my Maiden Entry. I just looked up and caught him smiling, so glad is he to have finally got the old duffer engaged upon some meaningful pursuit. Would that I had the skill of a Gilray or Hogarth to portray him in the margins of this work, a vain youth, stopping to admire himself before any passing reflection, standing sideways to better trace the cut of his trousers. I have even seen him, unaware of my presence, blow himself a kiss in the glass.

He nods that I should return to the business at hand, patronizing pup. I try scowling back but fear all the venom I pour into the look only raises it to the level of an old man's bluster. Such are the indignities of age.

How much more do I have to scribble here before I can decently close this volume, tuck it under my arm, and accidentally drop it in the Reflecting Pool?

He wants memories. I refuse to look back. The moment one looks back, one falls flat on one's face. To you, I may appear at the end of my journey, but for me the journey begins afresh with each step. The short climb from armchair to bed, for example, is an adventure fraught with risk, a perilous expedition that sets my heart pounding, screws my courage to its highest pitch, one that I intend to embark upon . . . now.

March 19

It appears to be morning. I say appears because, for all the rain beating on the windowpanes, I can make out only a grudging luminescence. I hate being trapped indoors. The worst of it is that, even should the sky clear later, the grounds will resemble a swamp, and with my leg continuing to worsen there is no way I will be able to take my customary ramble. So I sit, while Seabold amuses himself with a deck of cards. I had thought he was playing solitaire but just now he offered to tell my fortune, so I suppose he is dabbling in the juvenile mysteries of the Tarot. I could tell him a thing or two about the Hanged Man and the Queen of Cups, but with his hairs so carefully curled I doubt he would like to see them stood on end.

"Fortune, at my age?" I snorted. "I don't need a gypsy's mumbo-jumbo to tell me what lies in wait."

"Perhaps I will cast mine, then, although it is said the cards do not speak directly to the one whose fate they foretell. There is need of an intermediary."

"You shall leave when the roads clear and go to London. There!"

"By whose munificence?"

"Your sainted mother's," I answered evenly.

"Saints are not often in the habit of bearing children, are they? Although one could argue giving birth is the result of that ultimate martyrdom, for a woman."

I did not have my stick, but my fingers gripped the sides of the chair just the same, as if to thrash him.

"The funds you refer to," he went on, "have, alas, vanished along with the bubble in which they were invested."

8

"That was rash."

He had, the whole time, been laying cards out. Now he turned one over.

"Oh dear."

"I wondered what explained your sudden appearance. Filial piety seemed, from the start, a rather tattered veil to mask your true intentions."

"Not at all. You needed caring for. You still do."

"I need peace."

"Well," he gave an exaggerated look round at the portrait-choked walls and timbered ceiling, "if you cannot find peace here, Grandfather, I sincerely doubt you will find it anywhere this side of the grave."

March 20

He has gone riding. With barely concealed envy I watched him pull on his boots.

"Is it all right if I take Episkidon?"

"By all means. He needs the work."

The storm has reduced itself to a drizzle, but the vista from the terrace, where I have had a chair set out, is still that of an interregnum season, what is left when winter departs and spring has yet to arrive. The lawn seems a bare canvas. I imagine down by the Tym it is different. Swollen from rains, the river becomes swift and chocolatey. As a lad, despite warnings to keep away, I would roll up my pant legs or dispense with such encumbrances entirely and test myself against its current, stand first ankle, then knee, finally waist deep, bracing myself against that enormous brown muscle. It is amazing I was not swept away.

Is he simply waiting for me to die? I go over the facts and find that the most likely conclusion. The alternative theory, that he remains out of dutiful affection, is betrayed by his restlessness and mockery. Yet there are moments when I see in him . . . call it a spark of his mother, vying with darker elements for possession of his soul. I try to remember myself at twenty-one. Was I just as noxious a cad? I fear so. The question is: have I, in the intervening years, become a creature so much better?

These morbid reflections are the result of being served potted eel for lunch. I must tell Cook to scour the larder for items less unsettling.

March 21

Seabold did not return last night. I waited, first delaying dinner, then, afterwards, smoking a cigar in the library. When I finally heard the sound of a rider it was a boy from Greenwillows announcing that the Young Master, as the tenantry persists in calling him, met up with the Thomases in late afternoon, had been pleased to sup with them, and was now to be their guest.

Greenwillows! Well, if he is in search of diversion he can do no better than a visit with Squire Thomas, whose rustic brood no doubt kept him entertained till cock-crow. He is not back yet, at eleven o'clock the following morning, and so I find myself rejoicing in regained solitude.

My mother once said, "Billy, you are a queer lad, always shutting yourself up, engrossed in imaginary pursuits. Nurse worried about you, but I never did. It was Angela who was the object of our concerns, your father's and mine. You we regarded as a changeling, a visitor from some frosty clime, rather than a child it was our duty to raise."

I know not my reaction, if any, to these words when I first heard them. I do ponder their significance now. Strange confidence to make a child. And Angela, what on earth could they be concerned about with her? She was the cynosure of beauty for miles around. I still recall a dress she asked me to help her with—when I was young enough to be entrusted with such innocent tasks—that necessitated being sewn shut in back. God knows where her maid was. Helping with preparations, no doubt. It must have been our turn to host the Hunt Ball. I had never touched needle or thread before, and hear, even today, her laughing and crying out at my clumsy attempts to bind together the edges of taffeta.

"You are poking me," she protested. "You have drawn blood!"

. . . all while a marvelous scent rose. Which I wonder at, for Father did not allow perfume of any sort. Yet the fragrance, haunting and particular, has just traversed some eighty-odd years in an instant. If I followed my nose down that garden path, where would it lead?

March 22

A day has passed with no word of the boy's return. I will not lower myself to inquire as to his plans. I did take the opportunity, stumping through the moldering halls (it is raining again), to examine the contents of his room. Not, I suppose, a strictly honorable undertaking, and indeed, had I reflected before setting out, weighed the matter in my mind, I would no doubt have decided against it. The truth, however, was that I found myself in his chamber without a clear memory of having got there, gazing at the disheveled bedding (he has forbidden Mary, the girl, entrance) and a cacophony of strange tonics and elixirs arrayed round the washbasin. Several books, by authors with whom I have not the pleasure of acquaintance, were piled against a window where they had become wet. The atmosphere was one of dissolution. Proceeding further, I used my stick to poke at what appeared to be a lump under the blanket and discovered, to my horror, a silver salver reported missing several weeks past. At the time, a vagrant who had sought charity at the back gate was suspected. This led me to a more thorough examination of the premises which, while turning up no more missing valuables, did reveal a cache of letters from a woman calling herself Arabella. Here my sense of propriety returned, or perhaps it was distaste at the prospect of soiling my weary eyes further with proofs of the present generation's tawdry mores. For whatever reason, I quit that entire wing of the Hall and found myself, once again with no exact recollection of how I had arrived, at the stables, mourning the absence of Episkidon, the last, I fear, in what for so long seemed an unending procession of trusty mounts.

March 23

"Where do we go when we die?"

"We go nowhere. We open our souls to the Good Lord and He floods us with Heaven. It is our surroundings that become Divine. Our vision is cleansed by His Son's blood and we see, for the first time, eternal life in a blade of grass. Heaven is not some airy castle but a revelation that Time is the Devil's trick. One steps sideways, as it were, out of one's self, and sees all the old certainties collapse like a suit of shed skin."

My tutor held beliefs which, had Father known of them, would have led to his immediate dismissal. He used them as a kind of spur to encourage me in my studies. Latin, for example, which I detested, he pointed out contained clues to the Divine Presence in our everyday lives. Everything, indeed, obeyed a Law, hinted at a Pattern, was part of some Greater Scheme that ruled our stay here on this earth and so merited understanding.

"Not strictly orthodox," he agreed, when I pointed out how some of his positions seemed to challenge those held by the Vicar. We were walking through a meadow, slashing at the grass with sticks. "But you will find that *questioning*, rather than blindly obeying, leads to a deeper understanding of God than that obtained by those mumbling sheep grazing at their psalms."

"Then death is merely—"

"Quite," he cut me off. "Death is merely."

A daisy was separated from its stem and sent spinning to the ground. How young we were, the both of us, though at the time he seemed immeasurably older. I wonder how well that philosophy served him when, several years later, he was taken by fever.

March 24

Another day alone.

It is dark now. This journal proves a dangerous pastime. I liken it to a patch of quicksand, the blank page.

Turning, with an effort, my attention to the present, I must come to some decision regarding Seabold. He has lost his inheritance and shows no ambition, no resolve, to *get his life going*. This I must balance against the fact that he is my sole heir, young, and the product of a not untroubled youth, much of the blame for which lies with myself. To pack him off to London with vague notions of obtaining a Commission or being called to the Bar would be perfectly acceptable in the eyes of many and yet might very well be tantamount to sending the boy over a cliff. On the other hand, to keep him here and suffer his beady-eyed deathwatch in the hope his nature will gradually change over time into that of a responsible landowner is not doing the boy any greater favor. One can run through a legacy (if that is what one calls the paltry sum I will be able to pass down) just as quickly on a country estate as in Kensington or Regent's Park.

Shocking to realize that the boy's mother, at his age, had already left this world, and that *her* mother, my dear Wife—

Death is "merely"? Our own, perhaps. But the death of others only looms larger as time proceeds. Contrary to popular sentiment, one does not recover from such losses. The shadows of the departed lengthen as our life moves on. Years pass. These areas of darkness combine and thicken, until one has the impression of traveling perpetually through a graveyard, at dusk.

13

March 25

He is back. And has been pleased to bring with him a woman. Or women, rather. It is totally unacceptable. When I referred to Squire Thomas and his "brood," I still pictured them in their larval state, a jumble of writhing infants with no more marks of individuality about them than a colony of wood lice. Now they seem to have, in the blink of an eye, matured, the eldest alarmingly so. They arrived in the morning, when for the first time in weeks I had set out, carefully picking my way through the puddles, determined to get as far as the wood or, who knows, perhaps even assault the gentle ridge that borders the northern edge of the estate. An unmistakable neigh made me turn and there was Episkidon, unmindful of his rightful master, snorting and prancing with pride as Seabold led in a dogcart two females, one of them a lass of perhaps sixteen, the other a juvenile sister.

"Grandpater," he called, immediately setting my teeth on edge. "I see you are better."

"Better than what?" I growled. "I was in no-wise ill."

"Really?" he inquired, staying his horse and, with a gesture, halting the progress of the cart as well. "I sensed my presence was beginning to wear on you. That is why I hied myself away. And see with what treasure I have returned."

"Your Lordship," the girls giggled, both attempting some semblance of a curtsey, not used to greeting me from a greater elevation.

"Kate here was so kind as to see me safely home. I feel it only right to offer her refreshment."

"By all means," I muttered, turning to the comparative serenity of the forest.

In my day, which this is apparently NOT, urchins of small farmers would be permitted a wide-eyed intrusion of Upton at least once, to instill in them the proper sense of awe as befits a subject towards his master, after which they would only be allowed to appear outside the kitchen and beg for such scraps and sweets as Cook was kind enough to dispense. The notion of them, once they reached the age of common sense, penetrating the Hall by its front door, of their being offered lemon squash in the drawing room, was and still is, for me, unthinkable. I glanced back, when a safe enough distance away not to be observed, and saw Seabold helping the elder Thomas girl out of her conveyance. She displayed, not by accident you may be sure, a finely turned ankle. Her sister, still a brat, jumped over the rail on the other side, letting her skirts flap about.

Nature is a balm not appreciated by the young. Even the raw branches with their hard little buds, the dead leaves still miraculously clinging, having survived the winter (Survived? In what sense? Are they any less dead than their brethren trod underfoot?) gladdened my heart as I pushed through this spot of wild I have insisted on maintaining as a bulwark against over-cultivation. Marrow and cabbage, sheep and cow, may provide my grosser needs, but it is here I come for spiritual nourishment. I place my open palm against a tree trunk and feel just under its rough skin the same life force that pulses beneath my own, a sense of kinship I have rarely shared with my fellow man.

"Come!" I recall Angela shouting.

To make sure I would follow, she grabbed my cap, disappearing into this selfsame wood, these selfsame trees. I tore after her. Home from school for the first time, I noticed her in a different way, the result, I suppose, of spending so much time in exclusively male company; how she ran, her feet springing off the ground at each step, gaining a magical buoyancy from the soil, whereas we boys comprised a thundering herd attempting to pound the playing field into submission.

"I shall exact tribute!" I promised, using the slang of the common room.

Deep in what seemed a taller wood, I listened intently for the sound of her progress, fancying I was a colonial hunter in just-discovered America keeping an eye out for grizzly bears and the mysterious Red Indian. I crept forward and was surprised as she fell on me from behind, whooping with delight, pulling the cap down tight over my ears.

"Pax! Pax!" I pleaded, but fought back just the same, grabbing her wrists, surprised to find I could force them to the ground.

"William the Conqueror," she mocked, kicking me.

Then I discovered if I lay on top of her I could thwart that attack as well.

We both lay a minute, breathing heavily.

"Does Father still catechize you?" I asked.

She frowned at me and worked her hands free with a different kind of strength.

"I caught him in the hallway once," I explained. "He said he had been instructing you before bed. It is a pity they never got you a proper schoolmaster."

"Oh I am quite familiar with the ways of men," she said.

"But surely there are things even Father does not know."

"He knows All."

She made it sound a horrible fact rather than a vague word, a secret that now she, too, was burdened with. I tried resuming our horseplay but she slipped out from under me, got up, and began carefully readjusting her garments. Her long hair, in faint ringlets, was stuck with bits of leaf.

"Will you marry Albemarle?"

I was still lying idly on the ground, grabbing up handfuls of violets with the heedless destruction of youth.

"Who told you such a thing?"

"Price."

"Price is an ostler," she scoffed.

"But he knows All."

16

She smiled. I sensed I had made a joke without intending, one I did not understand.

"He does indeed." She bent over, gathering some of the pretty flowers I had torn, and put them in her hair. Now she towered above me. "What did Price say, exactly?"

"That you had met Lord Albemarle at the Devonshires'. That he and his father visited here, once. That Father and the Duke drank brandy."

"He seems remarkably well-informed."

"Is it true?" I persisted.

Then she did a queer thing. She removed her shoe and placed her foot on my chest. I lay there, gazing up at her. It was, I suspect, my first real acquaintance with Beauty and the sovereign power it can cast, most tellingly over its own possessor.

"I shall never marry."

"You could marry me," I hazarded, though of course I already knew that was impossible.

"That would present quite a set of problems," she said gravely, "for I must obey my husband in all things and how could I possibly take orders from you, my darling Pug?"

The gong interrupts my reverie. Although when did a mere reverie produce so much inked paper? I am shocked to find the hand that holds this pen a withered claw. Only a moment ago I was in the first flush of youth, teetering on the verge of some life-altering discovery, and now . . .

They are still here! The two females. Seabold is entertaining them, making them laugh in the sitting room as they wait for me to descend. I had assumed they would be gone by the time I returned from my walk. When it became clear they were not, I absented myself from luncheon, pleading indigestion, and resumed these journal entries in the privacy of my apartments. Surely by dinner, I thought, the country maidens will be on their way. But the hysterics he manages to make bloom in their simple souls penetrate even the oaken door of my study. Now the gong has rung again. I must quickly dress and face what promises to be an awkward evening.

March 26

It was, if possible, worse than I expected. Kate is a fetching child, English Rose in complexion, while Jenny, her younger sister, possesses the pre-moral nature of a wild cat, with none of that creature's God-given grace. She sat hunched before the full Sèvres service (which Mann had mistakenly laid out in the idiotic supposition our interlopers represented guests) as if the china itself were some trick or trap to catch the unwary.

"You don't eat off that," I said helpfully. "It is a lay plate. Mann will take it away presently."

"Is it a unicorn?" Kate asked, leaning over to admire her porcelain reflection.

"Rampant."

Seabold managed to give the innocuous word a lascivious connotation, mercifully lost on these lilies of the valley.

"It is our coat of arms." I heard, in almost inverse proportion to the rising anger I felt, a gentle avuncular sweetness in my tone. It was not, after all, their fault, being placed in such a false position. "A unicorn and three stars representing—"

"Oh Grandfather, they don't want to hear about all that."

He nodded regally as Mann swept up the plates and proceeded to ladle out the first course, asparagus soup.

"Is your father still experimenting with that Guernsey?" I essayed to either girl, not sure which would be more familiar with the master of Greenwillows' well-known adventures in husbandry.

This innocent question renewed, between the two romantics of the party, the laughter I had heard at the top of the stairs. Jenny, the youngest, scowled.

18

"We have not had guests," Seabold excused, "in the month I have been here. And Lord knows how long before that. So our conversational skills are, alas, a bit rusty."

He is nervous. He is . . . in love. It came upon me in that slow breaking way the sun dismantles a cloud. Re-examining the girl Kate, I could certainly see how even a callow oaf such as my grandson could seize on such a relatively unspoilt specimen as entrée to that world where all laws are altered and all colors shift. My heart was flooded with an equal admixture of pity and envy.

"He cannot mount."

"Eh?"

The voice seemed not to come from Jenny's mouth, which was sullenly facing the soup with ill-concealed disgust, but the top of her head, the line of plainly parted dark hair.

"He cannot mount," she muttered again. "The Guernsey. Father says he has an abnormality."

"That is not uncommon. Have they tried—"

"—lifting him, yes. The men grab his haunches on either side. But then Buttercup bolted, and Pluto tossed them off like so many flies. Lud, the stable boy, was almost crushed."

"That is my mother."

Seabold hastily pointed over my shoulder to the portrait. I did not turn to look with the others.

"She is beautiful," Kate gushed.

"Indeed she was. Or so I am told."

He shifted his gaze to me.

"Seabold's mother passed away when he was young, bringing him into this world, in fact."

"How awful."

A silence fell over us, which lasted until presentation of the squab.

"Cook has outdone herself," I finally offered, removing a small pellet that rattled against my remaining teeth.

"I was raised by wolves," Seabold explained.

"Wolfe," I corrected.

"Lord Wolfe, my father. And afterwards his sisters, Aunt Estella, principally. A jolly crew. I have always felt myself more at ease among the fairer sex."

"You were cosseted. The orphan."

"Well I was one, wasn't I?"

"We all become orphans in the natural course of events. You were merely given the opportunity to face your ultimate situation sooner rather than later, an opportunity you chose to squander by plucking that same tragic string over and over in blatant attempts to elicit sympathy."

The boy smiled. I would rather he threw down his fork and challenge me! Instead he seems to invite abuse, which a part of me—or a part not-of-me, since I have no control over its actions—is all too willing to dish out.

"He looks nothing like her."

The girl, Jenny, had barely raised her head the entire meal. The squab, as opposed to the untouched soup, lay neatly divided into piles of bone and meat, though I could not swear if any bits of the latter had passed her lips. They more resembled offerings, which would make her . . . an oracle?

"No," I agreed, once again refusing to consult the portrait. "He does not look like his mother. But in temperament he is every inch her son. The stubborn streak is unmistakable, distinct as a birthmark, as is his penchant for getting into scrapes."

"But how could he have gotten any of that from *her*," Kate frowned, "if, as you say, she never knew him?"

"Perhaps the very absence of certain qualities to rebel against instills those same traits even deeper in the soul. Or perhaps it is a trick of nature we have not yet fathomed, how one can inherit characteristics even when there is no benefactor to bequeath them."

"Perhaps my mother speaks to me."

Seabold gazed across the table.

"Perhaps," I nodded slowly.

The rest of the evening passed in a similar state of muted hostility. At one point I took him aside and asked how he intended to convey the girls home on such a pitch-black night. They were, he told me blandly, staying.

"Staying . . . in the house?" I sputtered.

"I have had Mary prepare a room. Jenny and Kate share a bed at home. I thought it would be more familiar to them if they did so here, as well."

"A room. Down the hall from your own, no doubt."

He looked at me, genuinely puzzled.

"It is a draughty old house. Full of sounds. I won't have them hearing ghosts, as I often did, during my visits."

"You were a child, then."

"Well the youngest is still, practically. As for Kate—"

"She is the daughter of a man whose father carted firewood. Either your intentions are unacceptable or dishonorable."

"My intentions are to safeguard her Virtue, which I saw was under siege at Greenwillows in a particularly nasty way. Really Grandfather, you know nothing of such things. You have led a sheltered life."

He spun on his heel and went to rejoin the ladies, whom we had left gawking at the parlour finery, dusty though it may be.

March 27

So it was that I discovered the boy's plan to turn Upton Hall into a boarding house. "For the time being," he assures me. He has already had me pen a note to Thomas retroactively inviting but, in essence, ordering his daughters' attendance here for the foreseeable future. At breakfast (the result of a secret compact he has made with Cook, no doubt) we were given eggs, buttered toast, and rashers of bacon. The girls, the young one in particular, shoveled this down, visibly relieved to encounter food they could identify.

Love. There is a section in *The Republic* where Sophocles, of all people, just happens to be walking by and, when asked his views on the subject, expresses relief "to be done with all that." He describes how before, in its clutches, he felt "a prisoner." Yes and no. While I am glad to make sober and sane decisions as to how I spend my time, no longer following a sprig of lilac attached to a bustle as I once did for an hour, without ever spying its owner's face, I must also confess to missing the spice of madness ardor brings in its train. Indeed love, for me (by which, make no mistake about it, I mean the coarsest male urge) is the most available portal to the Divine. Women— and ministers, whom I place just below women in the hierarchy of convention—chastise us for being animals, but I hold it is in those moments of pure bestiality that we are most completely our true selves. A man, when flooded with that sudden sense of need, has what the more genteel call a religious experience. And he has it in youth, even well into age, several times a day, not exclusively on the Sabbath, wedged into a pew hearing some eunuch in a dress gas on about virtue.

Now it is evening. Seabold is teaching Kate the rules of a newfangled game. He stands behind her, looks at her cards, then pretends to forget what he has seen. Meanwhile, Jenny regards the fabric of the chair she occupies, or rises and . . . paws is really the best word, touches various objects in a cautious, exploring way, with no intention of picking them up. It is as though she is apprehending them solely through surface. And I sit here, perhaps the most eccentric of all, mumbling as I scribble.

Where was I? Oh yes, love. And myself, what is it I feel now, no longer subject to God unexpectedly revealing Himself through a stranger's bewitching gaze? Like a bowl obscurely cracked though outwardly intact, I no longer "ring" when set down; rather I make a dreadful clunk. Something inside me has gone.

Seabold just allowed Kate to win the final trick. She is clearly delighted. With her victory? Or with his allowing her to have it? They are one and the same, I suppose. Jenny, making a methodical inventory of the curio cabinet, reaches out to touch an ornate silver mirror once belonging to my mother, then draws back her hand as if burnt.

Love . . .

March 28

There were nurses but I do not remember them. There was a nanny, Nanny Gates, but I do not remember her either, though I was told enough stories about the simple superstitions she held to have believed, for many years, that I did. But as I scrape away legend, which one is far more accepting of in middle life because it conforms to the crude approximations one then takes for truth, I am left with no real first impressions save those made by my mother.

Father was a fearsome, distant object, more an effect, like weather. He would storm and thunder through our lives, then depart, leaving us strangely untouched. I confused the hoof beats of his horse with the steps of his person, so often did he appear to me from on high, surveying the estate or about to lead the Hunt. Even his approach down the hall of the nursery, when those eruptions of temper brought him to the children's wing, was, in my ears, that of Genghis Khan and his Ten Thousand Mongol Warriors.

It was to Mother I ran, a safe haven which he sallied round, reigning in his anger, snorting and threatening, but definitely checked.

"Darling," I recall her drawling, when a nightmare chased me downstairs and I found myself in the strange adult afterlife of the billiard room, "what are you doing up so late?"

She smoked, a great scandal for a woman of that time, through an ebony holder. Her clothes were flecked with ash.

It was her indifference, oddly, that made me so fiercely attached. A cultivated *froideur* no doubt passed down through generations. Having so signally failed the test of parenthood myself, I find it difficult to blame my mother for whatever unhappiness she may have caused. Indeed, those small relenting moments when she acknowledged me, feeding me a forbidden morsel (as one would a dog, under the table) or bestowing a kiss of the utterly wrong nature, stood out as milestones, cataclysmic joys in an otherwise placid infancy. Would I have been content with a storybook mother laving me in common, dull-as-dishwater affection? I think not. Storybooks, after all, are storybooks for a reason.

When I was eight—it was that visit home after my first term at school—she took me down to the Tym and ordered me to take off my clothes. Though I had grown accustomed to being naked before several hundred boys, I hesitated, feigning a great interest in the muddy bank.

"Have you something to hide?" she demanded.

"If we are not permitted to swim, why disrobe?" I reasoned.

"You used to do both."

"I was younger, then."

"It is as I feared. They have turned you into a prude."

So saying, she stood up and—I argue this is not a true memory but the essence of the encounter, though it is now what I "see"—with a simple undoing gesture let fall all her garb at once. I turned as if from an overpowering glare and next remember her ankle-deep in the water, wading further with every step.

"Come swim with me, Billy. Come swim with me in the Tym!"

"But it is not allowed."

"Don't be such a stick. Come, be swept away! Until you have let the current wrap you in its arms, you have not lived."

What can I say? Rather than follow her, I ran. I ran and, in some sense, am running still.

After, everything between us changed. Where before there was holy indifference, that of a goddess towards her worshipper, now there was a mocking solicitude, a learnt, only-for-show, maternal "love" standing as rebuke to the unholy communion we once shared, to what she had offered me more explicitly, and I had so tremulously rejected.

March 29

These are not reminiscences. They are happening to me in the present. Had I cast a bucket down the same well even a month before I assure you it would have come up dry. What, then, has occurred to account for such a change? Seabold's presence? The arrival of Kate and Jenny? No, I refuse to believe my consciousness could be rocked so by mere happenstance. It is as if I am coming round again to moments I lived before. Perhaps life is spiral in nature. Forgotten periods of existence spring sharply into focus while others fade or lose what seemed their great import. Certain conditions magically reassemble themselves and with no warning one occupies the same spot one did eons ago while simultaneously remaining distant, gifted or cursed with a perspective previously denied. That distance, of course, is how far we have traveled, and so should give us a glimpse of the greater dimension in which all these briefly coalescing instants exist, the texture of time, as it were.

What highfalutin theorizing from a man whose only previously written opinions have been letters to the ____shire *Times* on the maintenance of hedgerows.

We are in the stables, Jenny and I. She runs her hand along Episkidon's flank. The creature's ears prick. He gives a strange meditative whinny, as if being consulted on a matter of grave importance. His milk-white side expands as her palm makes its slow progress.

I have brought her here to get away, though in doing so I am only encouraging the very progress that caused us both to flee. It is raining again and the ageless comedy Seabold and his rustic partner perform echoes through all precincts of the Hall. Wherever I attempt to encamp, the sound of their complicit giggles forces me to move on. Jenny and I are in some sense chaperones, I suppose, but it is not a role either of us relishes.

I cannot make out the boy's motives. Can he really be, as he claims, securing her virtue? One may as well rely on the fire to safeguard a refugee from the frying pan. If, on the other hand, his intentions are honorable, it would be a match so spectacularly crack-brained that I would have to intervene.

Clothes have been sent, along with a bushel of winter apples, from Greenwillows. Decent of Thomas. Jenny wears a dress that is clearly the product of two ancient gingham ancestors. Some cunning seamstress has managed to give what is essentially a meeting of scraps unity. As one follows daisies they become, without warning, white and red stripes, peculiarly apt attire for a girl who herself seems to straddle an invisible divide, becoming, from one moment to the next, a being quite other.

March 30

"Will they marry?" she asked, shortly after I had penned the preceding entry.

We were tucking into a picnic of bread and cheese, a most appetizing alternative to watching Seabold spear a forkful of game pie, or some other expensive morsel he persuaded Cook to make, and try maneuvering it past Kate's gaily laughing lips.

"No," I answered.

"Why not?"

"She is too far beneath him."

"Well she must be, mustn't she? For it to work."

I looked at her curiously.

"How old are you?"

"Mother says eleven."

"Mother says? Don't you know?"

She shook her head, button-faced, with very white skin and the beginnings of a pugnacious jaw.

"Most children do, don't they? Know their age?"

"They only pretend to. But how could they? I have no recollection of my birth. Do you?"

I considered that, then hazarded:

"Have you ever heard of Merlin?"

A questioning glance told me she had not.

"A wizard in King Arthur's day. He lived backwards, it was said. So he knew what would come to pass, but not what had been."

"He fancies her."

"Seabold? Fancies your sister? Yes, that is quite obvious."

"Not to him."

"Perhaps."

"You think because I do not remember my birth I am that wizard? Old what's-his-name?"

"Merlin. Of course not."

"How could I be him?" she demanded. "I am I."

March 31

Who released her when the Ball was done? Who took a knife to my clumsy stitches?

April 1

And who, for that matter, are *you*, reader of these lines conceived, I would venture to guess, before you were born? I feel your hot breath on my neck, hear your impatient fingers rustle ahead to see how much more time the old boy has got. Will he keel over in mid-sentence? Or will there simply be a commonplace observation about the weather followed by handwriting of a different sort— Seabold's no doubt, all backslant and curlicue—informing that his "beloved Grandfather" passed peacefully away on

27

such-and-such a date? And then, so eager to finish, what will you do next, man of the following century? Float in your aeroship to some distant galaxy for tea? Or, after puzzling at a language you can barely understand, rip this page from its binding, crumple it into a ball and feed it to the fire, as wind howls through remnants of a collapsed civilization and you cower before hungry animals whose eyes glow palely beyond the frail circle of light?

Yes, you came here to wallow nostalgically in the past, but just as I stumble again upon what was, perhaps I also glimpse, with a clearer eye than yours, the next bend in the spiral, that which lies in wait.

April 2

Unlike Seabold, I was troubled not by nighttime sounds but their opposite. After the fitful wheezings of six bunkmates, the Hall's deep silence grew oppressive. I lay for hours, listening to my heart pound, before finally creeping out, gliding through remembered passageways, and coming to Angela's door. She responded to my tap with the sharp voice of another who could not sleep.

"What is it?"

I let myself in and stood by her bed.

"You sleepwalk through the day and now dreamwake the night," she said dryly.

"What do you mean?"

"Never mind."

"May I come in?"

"In here beside me, you mean? No."

"But I used to."

"I have a new beau," she said. "You may lie on the floor, if you like."

I curled up on a circle of rug.

"Shall I tell you a story?"

"Yes, please."

"Once upon a time there were three ducks . . ."

28

The rug was a small craft, barely taller than the sea upon which it rode, a wafer-thin disc. I transformed myself into a smooth shiny ball and curled my fingertips over its edge to better keep from falling off.

"The second duck, a particularly bothersome mallard . . ."

The hoof beats of my father's horse rang through the dark. I was on the other side, away from the door, invisible to him. The voice I heard was not his usual snarl but deep and melodious.

"Angel," he called, "are you asleep?"

There was a pause. We both knew she was not. Her breathing had stopped altogether.

"Poor child," he murmured.

I do not know in what state I existed, where dream ended and reality began, but I was sure at that moment Angela waited to say a word, to draw breath even, until I had silently rolled my insignificant body the quarter-turn necessary to vanish under the bed. When I did, it was as if a genie had been released. There was a hiss of steam and distant, whispery cries.

"There, there," he comforted her.

I was no longer on a ship but in the sea now. Or the sea was in me. It roiled the pit of my stomach, sent waves crashing to each extremity. I felt a tidal push and pull as some force struggled to be released, while dust sifted down from creaking bedsprings and my lungs fought the urge to cough.

"My *angel!*" he cried decisively, consigning her to heaven.

April 3

Like those other newfound reminiscences, that night has never existed for me until this day. I am still leery as to its meaning. Perhaps it has none. Can one retrieve, from across the chasm of time, a mere *dream*? There is always the possibility I am going mad. I have witnessed such a descent firsthand and am familiar with its trajectory, how harmless quirks become, when viewed from the endpoint of the sick room, with its iron door, its leather restraints and male nurse, unheeded warnings; how, in the end, character itself, those immutable traits we hold define us, is revealed to be no more than a symptom of dread pathology, if not worse.

Resolved: to remember no more.

April 4

Seabold's interest in the supernatural has found a willing accomplice in Kate. Together they are experimenting with the ouija board, an excuse, I suspect, to touch knees, as the planchette skitters this way and that over the alphabet. I have found a book for Jenny, since her education appears to have ended just when it should have begun, with the ability to read. It is a fable written by my old Lecturer in Mathematics, about a girl who falls down a rabbit hole, or some such nonsense. But remembering what a fastidious man Dodgson was, I am sure it contains nothing inappropriate.

Here is what the spirit world has contributed to our evening:

LOV UPROCHES FLEA ALL DISBELEAVERS

April 5

Cook has been with us only ten years. I still recall when she applied for the position. She was of that indeterminate age widows affect, beyond pulchritude but not yet wrapped up in a shawl like the crones who frequent Saint Bartholomew's. A mature, somewhat stout woman with immoveable hair. I read over her letter of reference, offered belated condolences on the death of her husband (which necessitated her return to Service after an all-too-brief interlude of domesticity), then firmly laid down the rules of the Hall respective to meals: simplicity, punctuality, economy. I am no miser, but memories of waste, of the table resembling the scene after a catastrophic battle, with still-smoking, half-gnawed carcasses strewn about, waiting to be fallen on by footmen and parlourmaids, left me yearning for the beauty of a cleaned plate. In the decade since, she has proven an exemplary taskmistress to those beneath her, as well as an amusing source of gossip, seemingly oblivious to the vast social gap our respective positions demarcate. I sent for her this morning, while still in bed, my leg was throbbing so.

"It takes men that way," she nodded sympathetically. "By the end, my Joseph couldn't move but he'd scream."

"Your late husband had gout?"

"Oh no. Dropsical, he was. Your Lordship remembers. The leg was what done him in, though. Made him give up hope, I always say."

"I see."

"He just stopped fighting, he did."

She stands. I will nod for her to sit but she prefers to remain, like a soldier, at attention. Age has filled the outlines of her face and figure. I cannot conceive of her looking any different than she appears now. She has reached the point in her life she was destined to attain. Any subsequent change will refer to this ideal moment she quite literally embodies.

"The boy," I say, "has been discussing with you what is to be served."

"Master Seabold simply wishes to relieve your Lordship of the responsibility."

"I see no need to be relieved of anything. Choosing what I eat is hardly a burdensome task."

"There are the young ladies to consider as well. Two-day-old fowl and last year's potatoes are well and good for gentlemen dining alone, but—"

"They are not *ladies*. They are visitors from an adjacent farm. I daresay the meal you just described is more what they are accustomed to. It is this confounded attempt to treat their lingering here as some kind of Royal Visit that has no doubt aggravated my condition."

"Your Lordship's leg was bad long before Misses Kate and Jenny arrived. If you like, I could prepare a Concoction. Joseph used to swear by my—"

"Oh God, not another one of those."

"Say what you like. The doctor told me it prolonged his life beyond all measure. Told me that at the funeral, he did. Very nice of him to come. They don't often, you know."

"Have you any idea what he is up to, Mrs. Ellis?"

She wears a cap, more a ruffled sort of headpiece, really. I have never seen her take it off. But when she considers, she touches its sides with both hands, as if to remind herself it is still there.

"Up to? I suppose you mean with the eldest?"

"Of course I mean with the eldest. He tells me there is some sort of unpleasantness under her own roof that he is rescuing her from. Though how he managed to confuse himself with Sir Galahad I shall never know."

A shadow of concern flitted over her features.

"Is there any inhabitant of Greenwillows, some tenant farmer or hired hand perhaps, you could picture acting in an improper manner?"

"It is not for me to tell tales," she replied stiffly.

"Tales are not what I am in search of. What I require are facts, so as to be able to arrive at a decision."

"A decision concerning what?"

"That is my affair. All I am asking is if you know of anyone at Greenwillows who could conceivably pose a threat to a maiden's peace of mind."

"Col Woodforde." She made a face. "Cousin Col, they call him."

"He is a cousin of whom?"

"Evangeline Thomas. Her people are from Somerset. He arrived only two months ago, looking for work."

"He lives with the family?"

"In the stables, I believe. There is a room in back."

"And I take it the people here do not think much of his moral character?"

"It's said he is one of those men more upright lying down than standing up, if you take my meaning."

"I do indeed."

"But I have heard nothing of his forcing unwanted attentions on Mistress Kate. He would be a fool to do so. Squire Thomas has great plans for that girl."

"Nevertheless, Seabold's supposition may not be wholly without substance."

At the mention of his name, Cook reverted to our previous topic of conversation.

"The boy *has* been acting strange, lately, when it comes to the table."

"How so?"

"—said he wanted *vol-au-vents* tonight."

"Vollo-what?"

"Those French pastry shells, you know. I thought I would fill them with—"

"You will do nothing of the sort. We will have mutton."

"But the ladies, sir. It won't do to have them spatter grease all over their pretty dresses."

"Ladies be dammed! I know for a fact that mutton is what you were planning to serve before this mad boy put ideas in your head. You will not go confusing my kitchen with that of a Parisian bistro."

"Very well. But your Lordship has trouble chewing meat lately, what with his teeth becoming wobbly and all. Shall I mince it up for you?"

"Get out!" I roared. "Before I send you packing back to Lord Suffolk and his 'Only Foods Mentioned in the Bible' regimen."

This encounter, not at all untypical, fueled me with enough indignation to rise and dress. Despite my extra hour of repose, no one else appeared to be awake. I strode through the empty rooms, not caring if the loud report of my stick shattered another's sweetest dream. The lawn's

33

aspect, after several week's worth of rain, was steamy, boasting the kind of intense jungle-green that repels as much as it invites. Life, yes. Perhaps too much life. The kind of life one sinks ankle-deep in, if not deeper. Circum-navigating the verdant quagmire as if it were a huge man-eating plant, I stuck to the gravel drive and made my way to the start of the elm-lined avenue which leads eventually to the Old Pike and thence town. There, though, I could go no further. I poked at viscous, yellow-tinged slime.

"She quite likes you, you know."

Seabold, more properly shod than I, was leading not Episkidon but his stable mate, Fleur.

"The brat, you mean?"

"No. Kate. She idolizes you, despite my attempts to point out your—" he gestured with his riding crop since, humorously, metaphor had become fact, "—feet of clay. But she will have none of it."

"She is a fine girl," I allowed, then, after a pause, con-tinued: "Are you exercising her?"

"The horse, you mean?"

I sighed.

"Yes, Grandfather. Hadn't you noticed? I take them out alternately, each morning, despite the weather. Can't have them kicking down their stalls."

"Bully for you."

"I don't suppose you would care to join us on yours? Give the mare a run for her money?"

The feel of a horse under one, the extension of muscle and will, glowed intensely before my eyes one last time, then winked out, leaving a thin, smoky trail.

"Not this morning. Another time," I lied.

He pulled himself up onto the saddle and a moment later was galloping down the river of mud. Only when I turned back towards the Hall did the echo of his earlier words reach my ear.

Kate, fond of me? I wonder why. I have certainly not given her cause.

April 6

The first signs were, as I said, no signs at all. They only became so in retrospect. They were nervous tics, exaggerated perhaps, but easily explained away. Yes, he struck me with a poker, but it was more a barring motion as I unthinkingly moved past him towards the dining room while he made one last adjustment to the fire.

It was my own fault, I told myself later, examining the oozing welt on my shin.

"Your father is a strict believer in precedence," Mother reminded.

Meals were a rather somber affair, my parents being followers of a fashionable quack who believed all health problems could be ascribed to the inadequate chewing of food. With each bite they would count to forty before swallowing. Contrarily, my own recent introduction to the barbarities of the Dining Hall made me eager to stuff as much sustenance into my belly as possible in the shortest amount of time. I looked up from this frantic gobbling assault to find several pairs of eyes fastened on me.

"Tell us something you've learnt, William," Angela suggested.

"The death," my mouth was still full, "of Archimedes."

"Since I have no idea who the man was when alive, I don't see how his manner of death can interest me," Mother pointed out.

"He was the man who took a bath and shouted Eureka!"

"Oh, him."

"And how did he die?" Angela asked gently.

I noticed she was permitted wine now, a half glass diluted with water.

"The Romans were taking over the town in which he lived. They had been told not to harm him." I warmed to my subject. "But when a soldier entered Archimedes' house he had all these circles drawn on the floor. Some problem he was working out. He told the legionnaire, 'Don't touch my circles.'"

Mother had been chewing the whole time, staring at me.

". . . and so the soldier killed him."

"Served him right," Father muttered.

Now I recall Lord Albemarle was there as well, which is of course why I had been prevented from running on ahead. Father was touchy in matters of rank.

"I imagine the old school has changed a great deal since my day."

Albemarle's ease was what impressed most, a confidence particularly noticeable to a red-faced youth only recently permitted to eat with the adults, and equally attractive, I imagine, to a fifteen-year-old beauty not yet hardened to men's stares. Rather than take his food, he held it at bay, allowing only the choicest morsel, the most vinous sip, the honor of being consumed. Was he handsome? He was young, and rich. Ugliness, had he possessed it, would have become a quality of extreme desirability. And he was not ugly.

"Your father has an estate in Ireland?" Mother asked offhandedly.

"County Kerry," he answered with matching carelessness. "I have only been there once."

"Good hunting," Father grunted.

There followed a discussion of guns and slaughter in which I did not take part.

"Angela must show his Lordship the Glen."

"All sorts of game there. Snipe, woodcock, might even scare up a pheasant."

"William can be his bearer."

As we rose, I discovered my leg to be swollen, a deep tankard brimming with pain.

"What is it?" Father demanded, seeing me stand irresolutely and grip the chair.

The men, of whom I was apparently now one, were expected to segregate ourselves.

"Come, William." Albemarle practically scooped me up as he passed, putting my arm around his shoulder. "For the moment, *I* shall bear *you*."

April 7

And now the pain has returned. My cursed leg. It is the weather, of course. This wet.

April 8

I am haunted not by the past but by you, Reader. What are you doing here, wringing from my reluctant brain such sordid visions? Have you nothing better to do in your spurious future? Spurious, yes, because little has changed, has it? Perhaps your inkwell is replenished by some clanking automaton instead of a doddering valet, but do you not still gaze at the very air in front of you and feel an utter inability to apprehend *What is it?* this life we are handed, juggle for a time like a scorched potato, then let drop, all in the blink of an eye. We are one and the same in our predicament and our end. I labor under the lash of your expectation, yet can tell you nothing you do not already know.

Today, the boy rode longer than expected and returned covered from head to toe in mud. He had a bath drawn, which entails quite a bit of commotion, what with our antiquated pipes. I could not help noting a certain alacrity in the servants' steps as they scampered downstairs and up with various implements and linens. It made me surreptitiously sniff at my own frowsty clothes and wonder how long since the last time I

April 9

I fell asleep penning the above-written entry. They found me when I did not respond to the second gong and insisted I come to dinner without dressing. This made the contrast with our formal china, which Mann still insists on laying out, even more absurd. We were served pastry shells filled with a dainty sauce.

"*Vol-au-vents*," Seabold said helpfully.

"I know what they are."

"Cook's specialty," he explained to the girls. "She used to serve them when I visited."

Odd he refers to his stays here as visits. I was under the impression this was his principal residence, growing up, though I can see how in terms of duration and affection that was not strictly so. After my daughter's tragic end—a wound that, if anything, has grown more tender and unexplorable over the years—I could not, already a widower, envision raising a small child single-handed. There was, of course, the boy's nominal father, a swine masquerading in the uniform of Her Majesty's Navy. But Wolfe (despite his name, a pig) was at sea for long stretches of time and then, when Neptune answered my most ardent prayers, permanently. His sister offered temporary succor while I communed with my grief over Miranda's passing. This evolved into a shuttling of the boy back and forth until school formalized the arrangement to his spending each vacation with one of us or the other. But I never doubted for a moment he considered this his home. It angers me now to hear him state otherwise.

"Tell us something you learnt," I prompted.

I sensed, from the awkward silence that followed, conversation had been flowing unimpeded all around me, lost as I was in private thought.

"It was never clear," I went on, "what you did at school, besides drink to excess and run up debts. Oh yes, and be sent down. I should like to know what, if anything, you learnt."

Question: How does a boy become a man?

Answer: Through repeated kicks.

. . . or so I recall Father describing a dog being corrected of some reprehensible habit.

"I suppose what I principally learnt at school was that I was not cut out for the life offered me," Seabold finally replied.

"Cut out? Cut out? One is not a paper doll. One is a man. One grows, God willing, into the position one was born to assume."

"Perhaps in my case God did not will it so."

Despite his easy manner I could see sullen resentment lurking.

"And what does God will for you now? Do you intend to float—like some remnant of a shipwreck caught in the tide—for all time? When will you take charge of your fate?"

"My fate? How can I take charge of that which is by definition beyond my command?"

"By marching out to meet it on a level battlefield. By wrestling with what Life has in store for you rather than mutely accepting each turn of events as if it were preordained."

"You are too hard on him, my Lord!" Kate burst out, clearly shaken by the turn the conversation had taken.

I was touched. I saw what it cost her. Unfortunately, once the spirit moves me to speak in this vein it is very difficult to stop.

"He dazzles you," I rounded on her. "It is easy for him. It requires no effort. That is the appeal."

"Grandfather is not well."

"You would be advised not to believe what he says. He is toying not only with your affections but—worse!—with his own."

"Grandfather."

He had circled the long table and now appeared at my side.

"Not going to finish your 'fly in the wind'? That is what it means, you know." I spoke exclusively to the young ladies. "*Vol-au-vent*. Lighter than air, it is supposed to be."

"Let me help you to the sitting room."

"Why? I have hardly begun."

"Or perhaps you would like to lie down."

"I am the Head of the table. You are the Foot," I pointed out. "When, pray tell, does the Foot order the Head about?"

"When the Head suffers from confusion."

"She must have been younger."

We all three looked at Jenny.

". . . than you, I mean. If *she*," she nodded at the portrait, working out the dates, "died giving birth to *him*, and you are at least eighty, then your wife must have been—"

"Hush," Kate scolded.

"No, no. The child is quite right. I married late in life and my wife was considerably younger."

"Twenty years at least. Likely more."

"It is not uncommon."

Seabold was still standing, awkwardly now, like a waiter.

"If you don't like yours, Grandfather, I could ask Cook to get you something else."

"On the contrary." I took a bite. "I may very well have another."

The tension seemingly averted, he returned to his place. Jenny was still staring at me.

"Twenty-seven years," I finally said. "That is how much younger she was."

Mann came round with the wine.

"She?"

"Alice," I pronounced. "My darling Alice."

April 10

—struck me with a poker and then hissed "insolent-bastard-no-fruit-of-my-loins" in a voice so low only we two could hear. And Mother, of course, lounging on the divan, flicking ash in the general direction of the fire.

I can barely raise my leg.

I was not present for his more extravagant displays, though they are legend. His attempt to dam the Tym with nothing more than a gardener's spade and a copy of the Magna Carta. His insistence on eating, at one sitting, twenty raw eggs. The descent was rapid and terrifying. He soiled himself and used the filth to anoint his naked form. By then, Rodgers, the minder who had been recommended to us, was firmly in charge. I will never forget the combination of deference and contempt he showed. Even now it makes me look wildly about to assure that my own wrists are not in shackles.

"Gone done made a mess of ourselves again, have we, your Grace? Mustn't have that."

And then the groan. He had a special way of handling him, of hauling him up, that, while seeming to render assistance, was also punitive. A trick or gift for invisibly inflicting pain.

"You sit *here*." There followed a caterwauling scream, incommensurate with what took place before my eyes, yet the result, I could have sworn, of savagely intended pressure. "Visit with your boy a bit while I get Nurse Francis and a basin of hot water."

The restraints clicked in place.

Was there a pattern? I remember desperately seeking a pattern as a way of evading contact with his terrible eyes. Was he, with the stripes and daubs and speckles of waste, attempting to print some primitive message on his skin? Or counterfeit the markings of a zoo-bound beast? My back involuntarily felt for the wall, so earnestly and against my better nature did I wish to escape.

"Your father gets notions," was all Mother would say. "They buzz round his head."

That was as much as she could admit. Life went on as if he had merely moved his study to this attic eyrie equipped with padded walls.

He squinted at me through the haze of his illness.

"What have we here?"

"It is William, Father."

Despite being chained and degraded, he still had the power to make me feel the one worthy of shame.

"William. Come across to take charge?"

"No, Father."

"Think to make me the Old Pretender, do you?"

Oh God. William of Orange, I realized, coming across from the Low Countries to start the Glorious Revolution.

"It is William your son, Father."

"Well it won't do," he crowed.

"What won't?"

"On you, the crown will slip down. You are incapable of supporting it. You have not the cranial circumference. The gems will become a glowing jagged-topped wall surrounding . . . surrounding . . ."

He mimicked a prisoner's hopeless stare. Lost himself in the part. Gazed off. This was not uncommon.

"Father, our house eleven finished first this year. We are champions of the school."

"Sod them all," he murmured. "Not excepting your mother. Note I say 'your' mother, for I will have none of her."

Later, she would only go so far as to call him "dotty," and even this with a strange affection previously lacking in their intercourse.

April 11

Looking back over what I just wrote, I see I used the word "illness" to describe Father's condition, yet at the time I do not believe any of us regarded it as such. It seemed all of a piece, as if we were witnessing the trajectory of a spectacular meteor blazing across the sky. Indeed, if such conditions fall under a doctor's purview, why are they never alleviated? Does not a disease, by definition, imply a cure, even if it is not yet found? You, occupant of your ultra-modern age, do you still have men walking about with the fire of madness in their gaze? I would wager so. If no method of relief has been discovered over the whole history of mankind, then perhaps it should not properly be spoken of as an affliction. Perhaps it is simply a state of being. What he suffered from was elemental. That, at least, was how we chose to accept what had occurred.

"Usually it is a mad*woman* in the attic," Angela puzzled. "In stories, I mean."

"Things do seem topsy-turvy," I admitted.

We walked the Glen, so it must have been the following fall, since Albemarle was back and, at Mother's insistence, had set off with us on our long-delayed hunt. I held the second shotgun and had a bag slung over my shoulder that trailed along the shrubby soil. This was an affectation, that the Young Master (as *I* was then called) should play an ignorant bearer, all part of the Arcadian atmosphere courtship was thought to best thrive in.

"Does he speak to you?" I asked.

"Father? After a fashion. Why? Doesn't he to you?"

"Not really. He curses, mostly. Calls me names."

"Names? Of what nature?"

I stammered, unable to pronounce more than the first syllable.

"B-b-bas—"

"Oh!" She clapped her hand over my mouth.

Angela's beauty was now at its heartbreaking height. She had developed a stern look with which she tried counteracting the silly effect her presence had on people. I thought at the time I was immune, but now realize I was the one most completely under her spell.

"If he does not kill something soon we shall never get home," I whispered.

"It is best if you don't talk," Albemarle called, several paces ahead.

He scanned the clumps of green, the flat rocks where a trickle of water ran, with mild curiosity. Two dogs—how could I forget their names? Jezebel and Delilah—sniffed the ground and bobbed their heads, several hundred feet on.

"Will he ask Father for your hand?"

"If he does, I shall tell him to wear an old set of clothes."

"Or a smock," I giggled.

There was a brushing sound overhead. With one fluid motion Albemarle aimed, fired high into the air, and held out his hand impatiently for the other gun. Of course by the time I galumphed over to where he stood the remaining birds were gone.

"Hard cheese," Angela sympathized, as Jezebel returned with only one broken carcass and laid it at his feet. "William, you must learn to 'hop-to.'"

April 12

This morning, during Seabold's time of exercising the horses, I sought out the young ladies, finally running them to ground downstairs, of all places, where Mrs. Ellis had put them to work shelling peas.

"It is more what we are accustomed to," Kate explained, blushing furiously, her dress spread wide to catch the green casings.

I forbore any remark about "seeking their own level" here in the bowels of the Hall for the very good reason that I too feel more comfortable in its labyrinthine recesses. For one thing, the rooms are cozy, scaled back to the requirements of one or two workers, each intent on his or her task. It is also more immediately discernable what each chamber is for. The gun room. The coal bin. Upstairs, where I have been forced to pass the majority of my life, it was always less clear what action, say, a drawing room was supposed to, in the military sense, *contain*.

"So you asked to be given a job?"

"Oh no. We were feeling out of sorts. Then Cook came up to wonder why we hadn't touched our breakfast."

"She has been crying," Jenny translated.

I noted the younger one's style of freeing the peas from their pods was different than her sister's, more a dissection, again resulting in two carefully ordered piles so that one could not tell, from the care bestowed, which represented the desired and which the rejected.

"I have not," Kate pshawed, and then because—charmingly—she was so unused to telling even the tiniest of fibs, amended that to: "It was nothing, really."

"Is it because of what I said at dinner the other night? About the nature of my grandson's affections?"

"Oh no, your Lordship."

"Because I regret that. You seem a fine girl. Too good for him, in fact."

"Your Lordship is being kind."

"If anything, your presence here has had a beneficial effect on his character. You have made him speak and act more responsibly."

Her normally damask skin took on the blush of a ripe peach.

"Nevertheless, perhaps this crying spell means that you are homesick."

"Yes. I expect that's it. Although," she allowed herself a smile of exceeding sweetness, "many's the time I dreamt of being whisked away to just such an enchanted fairy castle as this."

"I should say *she* dazzles *him*," Jenny went on, "rather than the other way around."

It took us both a moment to realize she was still stuck on my outburst of a few days before.

"You must pay no attention," Kate chatted on gaily, her fingers tugging at a recalcitrant thread. "At home we say my young sister discourses with the Little People. Oh my!"

Several peas popped to the floor.

"No doubt you dazzle each other," I smiled, hoping that would do as an apology, feeling the need to right a wrong. "He has been corrupted somewhat by his brush with the outside world. I believe your innocence has gone a long way towards cleansing his soul."

This did not, alas, patch over whatever slight the young maiden was recovering from. Indeed, the opposite occurred. She burst forth with a fresh flood of tears and, scattering peapods, rose quickly to squeeze past me out the door.

"It is not Little People," Jenny scoffed, concentrating even more fiercely on her task, feigning obliviousness to the exhibition we had just witnessed.

"That you talk to?"

"It is to myself, of course. When I speak out loud, I speak to myself."

"Why is that?

"To better judge my thoughts. Once they touch air, the sillier ones wither away."

"I suppose adults find it easier to credit the existence of elves and leprechauns than a child your age having thoughts worthy of judgment, much less thoughts *about* thoughts."

"Is that what you think?"

"No." I once again smiled benevolently but she refused to notice. "Will your sister be all right?"

"She is not crying over anything you said."

"Why is she crying, then?"

"It is something he told her the other night."

"Seabold? What is it he said?"

"That he thinks she is grand."

"He told your sister she was grand? And that upset her?"

"She said it made her feel queer."

"Why?"

"I am sure I don't know." She finished the heap of peas she was working on and moved over to the next. "Maybe it is as you said, that she is too far beneath him."

"Is there anyone . . . ?" I paused, sensing the need to tread carefully. "Is there anyone back home who pays attention to your sister?"

She frowned, not understanding.

"Is there anyone who pays court to her?"

She extracted, in reply, a green worm, the same color as the pea into which he had burrowed, and dispatched it between thumb and forefinger.

46

"What about this Woodforde fellow?"

"Col?"

"I have heard he is on easy terms with your family. That he is some sort of relation. A distant cousin?"

"He is good with animals," she allowed. "They do as he says."

"What about people? Do they do as Col says?"

She looked up. Her eyes had a strange kaleidoscopic fervor to them. Perhaps it was because the rest of her features were still comparatively small, whereas those twin orbs had already grown to their mature extent, if not more so. They gave the impression of having been freshly recalled from viewing some vividly colored World beyond that of the ordinary.

"You cannot stop what is to be," she said, then gave an uncharacteristically modest shrug. "At least that is what I think."

"Stop what is to be? Why would I want to do that?"

"You can only stop what *was*." She nodded, as if in proof, to what lay directly in front of her. "Look."

"I see nothing."

"Look at your leg."

"What of it?"

". . . how it trembles."

April 13

"You know, Grandfather, you needn't write in that book all the time," Seabold hinted, suggesting my following of his own instructions was now to be seen as yet another eccentricity.

Everything we old men do subjects us to ridicule. It is especially true when we dare act human, reveal ourselves victims of the same frailties borne by others. That is when we are held to be at our most grotesque. The world regards us as monkeys, possessing only a cartoonish resemblance to those now in their prime. We, who were once their gods!

"I don't write in it all the time," I said mildly.

"You sit for hours, mumbling and scratching away." He stood, hands dangling, cravat hastily folded. Clearly he was waiting for me to pause. When I did not, he finally continued, "I need money."

I laid my pen down.

"What can you possibly want it for? All your material needs here are met."

"That I cannot reveal."

"And yet you expect me to—"

"All you need know is that I require funds, and since at the moment I find myself temporarily embarrassed . . ."

"Temporarily?"

"Do not, I beg, use this as occasion for some fiery sermon on my profligate ways. I would not have come to you if the need were not urgent."

"How much are we discussing?"

He named a not inconsiderable sum. Then, of course, I made the elementary deduction.

"This would be, I assume, to avoid the humiliation of a public ceremony?"

"I beg your pardon?"

". . . and so dispense with the obtaining of permission? Though I am sure Thomas would be all too happy to grant it. But I can see why you would want to do away with that excruciating scene as well. In a foreign town, no banns would be published and there would be no whispering to drown out whatever treacly organ music plays as you and your swollen bride slink your way down the aisle."

"Grandfather!"

"I assume there is *cause* for such whispers or you would not be acting in so hasty and underhanded a manner."

"I have no idea what you are talking about."

"Do you take me for a complete fool? Do you think I have entered my second childhood?"

"It does not concern Kate, if that is to whom you refer."

"Does she carry your child?"

His lip trembled with indignation.

"How can you even pose such an insulting question?"

"How can I not, when you two are practically joined at the hip, if not some more nefarious nether-region? True, she has only been here a matter of weeks, but no doubt you knew each other before. Oh, of course! Now I see. That is why you finally brought her to the Hall. For convenience's sake. What an ass I have been."

"There is absolutely nothing of that nature between Kate and myself. We are merely friends."

"Friends?" I snorted in derision. "You are not at school, Seabold, telling half-baked lies to an over-credulous don."

"And you sir, are not in the barnyard," he retorted. "All you ever think about are the Lower Relations. You disgust me."

"Wait," I called after his retreating form. "We have just begun our talk. What do you intend to do?"

"I was a fool to think you would help," he shouted back. "Confess it, you wish I had never been!"

April 14

This morning I finally summoned the courage to examine my leg. I have superstitiously avoided doing so until now, afraid of what I might find, suppurating sores or telltale swelling. But the ache remains bone-deep and shows no outward sign. Indeed, I wonder if the pain is physical at all, or brought on by these cursed memories.

I am still affected by Seabold's outburst, words he has no doubt already forgotten. The young do not believe they can cut us to the quick. We are the furniture of their lives, the scenery upon which they vent their frustrations, indulge their fantastic delusions. Our role is to remain mute witnesses, when not acting as unflinching recipients of abuse.

I must think this out, which I find increasingly hard to do in my head. Did I ever commit myself to serious thought before, or just react, much as a dog does, to scents and sounds, to stimuli masquerading as reason? Only recently, since I began this "mumbling and scratching" as Seabold described it, have I felt myself emerge from a lifelong fog. Perhaps it has to do with writing things down. Forced through the mesh of grammar, similarities are revealed, contradictions as well. Options are set in stark opposition. To wit:

It is clear, despite his pathetic denials, that he has gotten the girl "in a way" and is now resolved to carry her off and make an honest woman of her. This is just the kind of dunderpated gesture I can picture Seabold contemplating. For my part, I will do everything in my power to thwart his plan, for both their sakes. It is not scandal I object to so much as misery, the sanctioning of a misalliance that will blight its participants and their offspring for years to come. The oppressive weight of one's position here is a burden Seabold may, in time, learn to bear, but only with a helpmeet of his own class who has been similarly groomed for what they would face together. I have seen too many love-matches, fit subjects for poem and painting, devolve, almost immediately upon quitting the altar, into fiery Dantesque visions of Hell.

But if I refuse him the money, what then? The novelty of paying court to a commoner will quickly pall. And does he really think she, who has seen more in the realm of Lower Relations than he (with his expensive, cloistered education) can even imagine, believes any twaddle he may have spouted about "passionate friendship" or some other such phrase gotten from a book? He will move on, breaking her heart messily as he would a soda cracker, and with as little thought. Disgraced, she will then be sent off by her family to suffer among strangers, perhaps never to return. A budding life, ruined. That I cannot permit, either.

What, then, is to be done?

April 15

After a sleepless night, I have devised a plan of action, albeit an unconventional one. I dare not commit it explicitly to paper for fear it will resemble the ravings of a lunatic. Nevertheless it is quite brilliant, in its fashion.

I am just back from his room, which was little changed since my last visit, unless one counts a forgotten lump of what was once cheese that has taken on a life of its own. I had no trouble again finding the packet of letters from "Arabella" and this time extracting from them an address. Now the sole task remaining is to compose a wire in Seabold's name and have Mann slip away to send it unnoticed.

I am well aware this little scheme tampers with the lives of others to an outrageous extent, but now is the moment to test the powers of clarity and wisdom I feel suddenly gifted with. I cannot let him continue blithely down the road to ruin without at least attempting the kind of sage intervention I myself would have so benefited from, once upon a time.

April 16

I do not know when Albemarle first showed me his penis, or, as he vulgarly called it, the Member from Birmingham. Like so many events, it only seems odd in retrospect. At the time it was simply one more thread in the fabric of things, certainly not the most striking. The laurel for that would have to go to our talks, which I anticipated with dread and fascination.

"Not down yet?" he would ask, as we waited for the ladies to return after dinner.

I cannot credit how formal we were, actors enslaved to repeat a drama decreed by a man locked in a padded cell some three storeys above. He placed in my hand a whiskey and soda. I regarded the fizzing cauldron as if it were a wizard's smoking brew.

"I detest drinking alone," he explained. "You are . . . eight?"

"Nine," I answered, not knowing if I was allowed to set it down, thinking the turmoil taking place in the glass might have to do with my fingers, their pressure or heat.

"At your age I used to sneak it." He threw himself into a chair and looked about, clearly bored. "What do you think, William? Shall I marry your sister?"

"You must ask," I pointed out. "She may say no."

"Then I should be your brother," he went on, ignoring my objection. "Would you like that?"

I peered into the tiny circle and saw my reflection, all pockmarked with bubbles.

"You may approach," he murmured, lazily undoing the buttons.

It was a game. That was how he proposed it and that was how I took it, without either of us saying a word or addressing the situation at all except in the most facetious tones. It was like being back at school and so, as I said, hardly an incident worth noting. I do recall, afterwards, gulping the whiskey and soda, whether to efface the memory of what had just happened or to more firmly fix it, I cannot say. He wore rings. It was quite common in those days. They would inevitably catch and snap off small clusters of hair, stinging my scalp. That is the only "sensation" that has navigated the ensuing passage of years.

"Still the oak tree?" he resumed, as if he had been lost in private thought, clasping his hands behind his head.

"Oh, yes."

"Vickers used to beat me there."

"Vickers?"

"The Games master. I suppose he is gone." A look of melancholy softened his features. "You have no idea how quickly it all passes."

My tongue coiled restlessly in my mouth, seeking words to form, some lie to keep his wandering attention focused on myself.

"Where would you live, if you married Angela?"

"In Town, of course. I doubt we shall descend on this godforsaken spot any more than is necessary. You could stay with us over holidays. Would you like that?"

"I suppose."

"I make the offer because you seem ill-at-ease here, as if it were not your true home."

"Do I?"

"Sometimes you even act as if this were not your true family. Why is that, William?"

"Because they are unnatural."

I do not know how it came out. He was not interrogating me. He was simply making conversation. And yet it was the only thing I knew I should not say. Perhaps the liquor had clouded my judgment, though I think not. I knew, as children do, the exact extent of the evil I was performing. I remember the thrill of great guilt.

"Unnatural, how so?"

"Well, you see how in Father's case. He is mad, though no one will say it. And then there is Mother. She acts as if nothing is wrong, which perhaps makes her madder still. Just the other day she spoke of him attending the next session of the Lords. As for Angela . . ."

"Yes? What of Angela?"

I could not. I could not take that final step. But the harm was done, the suggestion made.

"And what, for that matter, of you, Billy-boy?"

I shrugged.

"Do you claim to be cut from different cloth? Are you the only sane denizen of Upton Hall? Is there no streak of noble inspiration in you as well? Or are you merely a dull lad and proud of it?"

He reached out with one finger and sealed my lips shut, running it along the line they formed, gluing them together so tightly, with such magic power that, a moment later, when Mother and Angela rejoined us, I discovered myself incapable of uttering a single word.

April 17

Some *lie?* The word, I notice, looking over what I wrote yesterday, inserted itself without my even seeing. I say I cast about for some "lie" to hold Albemarle's attention. Was it all, then, a fiction, my vision of the family as a group of writhing grotesques and I as the disapproving schoolboy holding himself primly apart? Was it all a monstrous exaggeration, borne of twisted jealousy? A nasty child telling tales?

This is the trouble with writing things down. One thinks one is getting to the bottom of it all, but Truth, by the light of a flickering candle, appears as variable as how droplets of ink choose to comport themselves on the page.

April 18

The weather having taken a turn for the better, I ventured out this morning to put the second part of my plan into action. By judicious use of my stick, I traveled quite some distance from the Hall, fleeing the swampy lowlands by following a natural rise that echoes the curve of the river before descending into another valley that extends beyond the limits of my domain, to Greenwillows.

Despite the sense of duty urging me on, I paused and considered how much more sensible it would be to turn and retrace my steps rather than struggle further, a good mile at least, to visit a neighbor with whom I maintained barely civil relations. However, there was no real question of turning back, and so I plunged down the treacherous slope.

Thomas is a go-getter. I remember him as a lad riding atop his father's cart, ostensibly keeping any stray faggots of wood from falling off, but more noticeably wearing a lordly expression on his face, master of all he surveyed, taking on both the viewpoint and manner of One Who Has Risen. This became a not inaccurate description of what he subsequently proceeded to do, coupling an indefatigable pursuit of wealth with a businessman's shrewd judgment of character until he had amassed enough capital to purchase several bits of adjacent land, rechristen them Greenwillows and himself "Squire."

Though our dealings have suffered no outward break, I am careful to maintain a certain distance, quite aware what a coup it would represent for him to be perceived as existing on anything like equal footing with myself. This is not due to a personal dislike. Indeed, I cannot regard Thomas as a person at all, rather as a representative of the noisy, meddling, striving class intent on destroying the world in which I was raised. Such feelings aside, he has proved over the years an exemplary neighbor, careful to respect my borders and rights of way. And now we do have a subject of mutual concern to discuss: that of our respective charges.

With such thoughts, I traversed the remaining distance and emerged from the wood directly in front of his barn, where he happened to be ordering several men to hold down a squealing pig.

"There!" he called excitedly, to which of the rude mechanicals I could hardly imagine, as both were struggling manfully to keep a grip on their muddy prize. "Two four six eight *nine*! Now how odd is that? It is what the Fancier's Handbook calls 'a supernumerary nipple.'"

His fascination with breeding is that of a dilettante. He has stocked his stalls with well-known oddities. There was even, several years back, a bison, though it died.

"The only odd thing is her survival," I opined. "They usually kill one with the wrong number of teats, turn her into the runt of the litter."

He is a round man, very bouncy. I saw from the way he gaped that my appearance had suffered from tearing through the supple, whip-like spring branches.

"Bless my buttons," he exclaimed, "it's his Lordship."

This momentary diversion was all the sow needed to make her escape. As she trotted off, the men in hot pursuit, Thomas advanced on me as he would a figure in the midst of falling, though I felt fine.

"I am here to see the Guernsey," I announced.

"His Lordship must come inside."

I could feel his grip, from a distance, offering unwanted support.

"Surely you don't keep bulls in the parlour." I attempted to shake off such a presumptuously over-familiar greeting. "Unless you have opened a china shop."

I laughed, amused at this sally, but also aware that what I said did not appear to be reaching the surface, as it were, but redounded on my person alone, where it set off contradictory ripples in my brain. Not the Guernsey, I objected. Not the bull. What am I talking about? Who gives tuppance about the bull?

"—cannot tell you how grateful Mrs. Thomas is," he was babbling, guiding me past the ordure and a modernized milking station. "The girls. So kind. Our flower. And the younger one, of course. First time she."

"Jenny!"

Her name alone, bizarrely, broke through the wall that seemed to exist, to have been erected in an instant, between the world and my powers of speech.

"Mind that hole. Did his Lordship receive those Cox Orange Pippins we sent, along with the."

Old Testament, I suddenly thought, glimpsing tottering legs, emaciated figure, sensing ragged, unkempt beard. My stick! With a bolt of fear I realized it was gone, and that Thomas was guiding me, steering me, disregarding both my will and whatever yawps escaped my spittle-stained lips. Old Testament prophet. Gibbering fool.

"Evvy?" he called, when we were still quite a distance from the house. "Evangeline!"

And so here I sit, ensconced no doubt in the same room Seabold was given during his visit to this way station for the despairing. When I grunted for paper, the urgent need overpowering whatever paralysis had shut

56

my jaw, they must have assumed it was to write notes, communicate wishes I could not make audible. But I quickly disabused them of that notion, watching my hand scrawl in large loopy letters GET AWAY FROM ME YOU BUXOM HOSTESS when Mrs. Thomas attempted offering a clay cup of water.

Doctor Rosewater has been summoned. I do not see why. This is clearly a case of over-exertion. Were it anything more serious I would not be able to record the events leading up to it, as I am doing now. These coarse sheaves of foolscap can be jammed into the book when I get home. They will make a fine lump in what I had begun to fear was too homogenous a volume. Surely one's Life, even the pages it is written upon, should boast a modicum of variety.

April 19

It has been many a year since I spent a night away from the Hall. Rosewater did not come until late afternoon. He entered just as I was penning the last entry and took a seat, observing in that shrewd way of his.

"I fear you have been brought here for nothing," I attempted to sigh. What I heard come from my mouth, though, was a shocking string of expletives punctuated by the phrase "confounded Christ-killer."

Having the grace, or perhaps long experience, not to take offense, he subjected me to the usual humiliating examination. I was puzzled at my outburst, which bore no relation to the words or sentiments I had wished to convey. With more care, I once again attempted to explain how an unwise bout of over-activity had led to my—

"Your Lordship," he interrupted a new salvo of curses, "has had a mild syncope. A brief interruption of blood flowing to the brain."

If I say the opposite, I cunningly supposed, perhaps that will turn the tables on this strange imp perverting all my utterances. Therefore, with great effort, I tried shouting, "Blast God!" and was gratified to hear my voice ask what treatment existed for the condition.

"Bed rest," he said, rummaging through his bag. "At least a few nights here, before you are allowed to move. And these drops, if you have trouble sleeping."

"Pudendum of Venus!" I mentally riposted, which somehow became, in its passage from brain to throat, a query as to what medicine he was giving me.

"Tincture of opiate. Five drops with a tumbler of water. Your grandson is residing at the Hall now, is he not?"

"I wish to die!" I said quite clearly, thinking, with muddled logic, that this similarly obscene thought would be transmuted to a simple murmur of assent.

Oddly, however, those very words were what my lips chose to echo through the homely master bedroom in which I had been installed.

Even Rosewater paused.

"Though the effects of such an incident may be—are," he corrected himself, "unsettling, there is no reason to think you will not make a full recovery. I was noting just now your motor skills, how you have retained the ability to write, which bodes well for regaining the full use of both body and mind."

"The Devil," I gasped, forgetting or too confused to try outwitting the tide of cloacal phrases clustered on the tip of my tongue. "The Devil's filth take you, man!"

He busied himself preparing a draught of the soporific he had just prescribed. I grew increasingly agitated. But it was not the news I had been given, nor the frustration of having my voice absconded by a dastardly ventriloquist, that made me shake and redden, stare bug-eyed from my propped position on the Thomas conjugal bed. No, it was what I recognized Evangeline Thomas had brought me the cup *on*: the silver salver from the Hall, the one I spied nestling under Seabold's coverlets, here now, at Greenwillows.

"If your Lordship drinks this, many of his symptoms will be alleviated. What you need is rest. Any further excitement may overtax your faculties."

The smell of laudanum. It is not the first time that poppy-sweetness has appeared in my life. I swallowed it, along with the grim knowledge its presence foretold. Previously, I had watched its magic properties work from without. I had stroked a clenched fist, soothed the tendon-stretched neck of one in excruciating pain, waiting for the drug to take effect. Now I felt the unholy cessation that all my loved ones must have experienced as well, a rapid distancing from quotidian cares. It brought me closer to those who had gone before. My eyes fixed on the salver's elaborate traceries, but rather than indignation at a precious heirloom bartered (For what? the question presented itself on the outskirts of my thought), all I did was bathe in the gleam of late sun on beaten silver. A fitting Last Sight.

sans date

. . . and then to waken, not knowing where or even who I was, with no light, not even a clear concept of what could provide light in the black blank world I had been transported to, my soul, my soul alone, for my body felt as if it were a dried-out husk ready to tumble aside and leave forever at the slightest spiritual twitch, at a mere—dared I hope it?—unfurling of wings.

"Alice?" I croaked, imagining that to one's wife would be delegated the task of welcoming a newly-crowned member. When the darkness offered no response, I tried whispering, with creeping dread, her name once more, fearful I had not, with all my latter strivings, made up for the missteps of a troubled past.

A match was struck and Beelzebub's head appeared, or so I believed for one terrifying instant, before Rosewater, holding a candle, leaned closer to peer into my eyes.

"Can your Lordship try saying something please?"

"The wages of sin . . ." my tongue formed thickly.

"Yes?"

". . . is death."

"Quite so," he smiled. "Your cerebellum already seems to be making the necessary repairs. And your pulse is strong."

I looked down. My body was still there, the flesh falling away from the bone like a mess of steamed fish.

"You have been here . . . ?"

"Just the night. You called out several names. A Doctor Meriwether?"

"Your predecessor."

"Ah yes. Twice-removed, I believe. More an apothecary, from what I gather."

"A butcher. He watched Seabold's mother die!"

Rosewater restrained me with a single hand. My body, come back to uneasy conjunction with its consciousness (we occupied the same spot but did not yet seem to have commingled) ached all over, the familiar ache of a fall, I now dimly remembered, of being pulled too fast down a hillside and smashing face-first into a tree.

"The event appears to have been mild," he went on, "although there may be residual effects. Rest is the only cure now. Would you like another draught?"

"No." I shuddered at the memory of a looming vision. "Gates. I was before the Gates."

"Were you? Of which place?"

I tried stoking my anger that a lowly physician should posit even the idea that I would not immediately, upon accomplishing my corpse, shoot heavenward like a flushed partridge, but there was not enough vitality in me even to form a frown.

And now he is gone. It is almost evening. It has taken me hours, hand dragging pen across this loose packet of paper, to recount what happened. Indeed, the feeling is more one of excavation. I brush aside bits of stone and dirt in my quest to discover the outline of what remains, a bleached skeleton, bones of the past, whether they be from the last forty-eight hours or forty-eight years.

60

April 22

"The Devil sometimes chooses to do battle with the mightiest among us," Canon Tillyard attempted consoling me upon Father's death, "to prove his terrible strength, while letting we more timid souls be."

But am I not the more mighty for staying sane? That was what I should have said to the man whose bread we provided in return for such watery comfort. All around me people were handed plaudits for living their lives, for embracing whatever dark fate awaited them, while I made way, made allowances, accommodated their extravagant excesses.

And now, when they have all burnt themselves up, left nothing behind but ash, I find my life gone too, without ever having taken a stand or dipped even one toe into the notorious "passions" so outwardly reviled, so secretly admired, of my kin.

His passing was not at all in the fashion one would have expected. "Peacefully," the announcement read in the *Times*, "surrounded by his loving family." No raging at the bars of his cell or improvising a noose from the soiled but still monogrammed sheets, as we had so long feared; merely word, delivered one day at tea, that his Lordship had failed to rise from his nap. Mother, opening her mouth to take a large bite of crumpet, paused, unwilling to retract the gesture but sensing some sort of response was in order, and finally motioned for Nurse Francis to take a seat. I can still see the poor woman, in her nun-like garb, shrinking to avoid contact with the very upholstery, so unused was she to take her ease before us.

"The doctor has been sent for?" Mother resumed, having chewed the requisite forty times and cleansed her palate with a sip of Fortnum's Darjeeling Blend.

"Yes Ma'am, as soon as we discovered him."

"Billy, you have not touched your petit four."

I obediently raised the sweet to my mouth, though it had become, in the course of so short a journey, alien and repulsive.

"A general decay of the faculties, I fear," Mother went on. "It runs in the family. A curse whose power I attempted to break by taking certain measures, though in doing so I was only half-successful, and at such a cost."

It took us a moment to realize what she said made no apparent sense.

"Mother," Angela breathed, and went to kneel beside her.

Albemarle took on the role of the responsible male and hurried the nurse away, going up to consult with Rodgers and wait for the doctor. I remained holding my petit four, examining how the moisture of the air had congealed into droplets on the sugary frosting, how on one raisin microscopic creatures were crawling, their tiny forms and even tinier legs engaged in a ceaseless round of activity.

There seemed to come from beneath the floor and behind the walls a quiet sobbing, a seeping tide of tears, as word spread among the servants. It was only here in the very center of the Hall, where we, the most affected, remained practically frozen in our respective poses, that no outward sign of grief was visible.

"M'lud?" someone called.

Steele, whose thick Liverpudlian accent was never adequately explained, stood in the doorway. I waited for him to be apprised of the dread news and turn away in sorrow, but instead he remained, an insistent presence, repeating:

"M'lud?"

Mother and Angela looked up. Their eyes, however, did not turn to the livery-clad figure.

"M'lud," he emphasized, a third time, clearly waiting for some sort of acknowledgement.

It was only then I realized that the object of his summons was none other than myself.

April 23

Unable to pass up a natural advantage, Thomas entered my room this morning "to see how his Lordship was doing."

He apologized for the humble accommodations and described an elaborate building plan that would practically double Greenwillows' present size.

"Your charming thatched cottage will one day rival the Hall itself," I smiled, "parvenu weasel."

"Oh no, your Lordship." He gave a worried glance. "Nothing so grand. It is only because the Missus and I have been blessed with such a lot of little ones, as well you know."

"All I know of your 'little ones' is that they possess large and unrelenting appetites, parvenu weasel."

There is always the shadow a sentence casts, what is left unsaid, what exists by virtue of its concealment. I found I had trouble now, not so much in forming my words but in excluding those sentiments that served as their ballast. The worst of it was I could not tell what traveled beyond the portal of my lips and what I managed to draw back at the last instant.

"That is exactly what I meant to talk to you about. The next generation, as it were. Our young ones, yours and mine."

"It is the very reason I set out to visit you in the first place."

"Really!"

"Indeed."

Drawing up a chair, he set it back to front, leaning on the wood until it gave a warning crack.

"They seem to be spending a great deal of time together," he began.

"Entirely too much time. And now the situation has come to a head."

"Has it?"

"There is no need to beat about the bush, Thomas," I snapped. "We are both men of the world."

"I am afraid I do not quite understand."

"I am willing to help out. Shoulder my share of the burden and all that. Never let it be said I was not a good neighbor. Surely there are candidates, men of decent standing and honest temperament, who would be willing to take a distressed soul to their heart and grace her with their Christian name . . . in return for certain pecuniary considerations."

He affected to be confused.

"When I said 'our young ones' I was speaking of—"

"Do not, please, gum up the workings of this aged brain with all sorts of petty details. Whomever you choose to stand as the strapping yeoman groom will be fine. I leave that to you. But I will *do my bit*. That is what I came here to say. That and no more."

"Your Lordship misunderstands. I wished to discuss my daughter Kate and the Young Master, not one of our tenant's girls who may have gotten herself—"

"In France, one kept one's hat on the whole time," I complained, feeling increasingly restless.

"France?"

"When the King of France deigned to stay in a noble's chateau, its owner, whether Count, Marquise, or even Duke, wore his hat indoors, to symbolize that he was no longer at home, to represent how all his possessions were held only in trust for his one true Sovereign."

"I see."

"Do you? Yet you come in here trying to take advantage of my weakened state, confusing me with all sorts of hinting talk, casting aspersions on my grandson—"

"Aspersions, my Lord? I cast no—"

"—when all I have tried to do, in journeying here and accepting your rustic hospitality, is the Honorable Thing, a concept with which you seem to have very little acquaintance, parvenu—"

"Grandfather!"

Thomas nearly toppled out of the roundabout chair as he tried lifting his chubby legs. I suppose it was awkward, the possibility that Seabold had been watching as we circled each other, venerable wrestlers, with his fate lying on the ground between us. But embarrassment is an emotion I have had little truck with, not for the past fifty years or so. One makes a gaffe, blunders, commits a "floater," and what of it? So long as one's intentions are sincere one can only fare forward.

"Master Seabold," he kept repeating. "Why didn't one of the girls tell me?"

"Perhaps because you haven't got any left," I suggested. "Girls, I mean. Perhaps because he has collected the remainder of your female offspring and distributed them among the various rooms of the Hall."

"Ah-hah-hah. His Lordship is making a jest now, is he not? I had trouble following you at first. He seems," he went on privately to Seabold, in a whisper worthy of the stage, "somewhat muddled in his thinking."

"I came as soon as I was permitted. Doctor Rosewater advised me to wait several days."

"You must be thirsty after your long journey," I said expansively. "Come closer, dear boy. Have some of this fresh water Mrs. Thomas has been so kind as to provide. Note the beautiful tray it rests upon."

"Kate and Jenny have come as well." He turned to Thomas. "That is why no one informed you of our arrival. I did not want to interrupt a tearful reunion in the kitchen."

Oblivious to all ceremony, Thomas rushed out to hug his girls. Seabold methodically turned the chair around and sat in it the proper way.

"Something about that man I don't care for," I muttered.

"Who, Thomas?"

"Shifty fellow. Don't know where he stands."

"At the moment he stands outside his own bedchamber, which he has ceded to you, a neighbor in need. Surely you could afford to be a bit more charitably-minded."

"Charity?" I glared at the salver. "He already appears to have received enough of that from our quarter."

"How are you, Grandfather? How do you feel?"

"Betrayed."

"By your body?"

"By my kin! Going behind my back as you have done. Selling your birthright for a mess of pottage."

"I cannot tell if you are raving or merely being poetic."

"Don't you see? You have declared your intentions by going to Thomas for the money I refused you, as if he were already the father-in-law he is so determined to become."

"How do my dealings with Thomas reflect on whatever I may feel for Kate? One has nothing to do with the other."

"Don't be a fool, boy! If a man is willing to steal from his own kind, and then take his ill-gotten gains to the father of the woman he wishes to run off with—"

"Please do not continue in this fantastic vein. I am not running off with anyone. As for the salver, it was my mother's, and so mine. I stole nothing."

I paused. In point of fact, he was correct, the salver having been given to Miranda on her wedding day. In the confusion that followed her death, most of the child's belongings remained at the Hall, which she herself had never really left.

"I took it as a keepsake," he continued, visibly embarrassed. "I imagined perhaps her reflection from long ago lingered there and so could mix with my own. A whimsical fancy, no doubt, but I have so little to remember her by. Then, when there was such a to-do over it being missing, I concealed it rather than be caught out, which I admit was foolish. But surely what I choose to do with my belongings is my own affair. In regards to your other bizarre accusation, when you refused me the money I had no choice but to offer Thomas the salver instead."

"Offer it to him for what?"

"A service he did me. One he was willing to perform gratis but that would have cost him a considerable amount. When I was unable to raise the cash, I felt duty-bound to give him the plate in compensation, payment which he accepted quite unwillingly, I might add."

"A service of what nature?"

"I cannot say."

"What possible service could a man such as Thomas render the Young Master of Upton Hall?"

"That is precisely what I cannot discuss. Neither can Thomas, which is why I interrupted you just now when—"

"Believe me, Seabold, Thomas considers any request you make of him, no matter how innocently motivated, a presumption on the marriage settlement he will one day make over. I am not surprised he accepted your payment 'unwillingly.' To him, it is reward enough how you are bellowing your desire for his daughter to all and sundry."

"That is absurd. 'Bellowing' indeed. I am no animal."

"On the contrary, to him you are a prize catch. He thinks you occupy the crowning page of his Fancier's Handbook."

"So good to see you back in form, Grandfather," the boy sighed. "You have no idea how worried we all were when you did not return that afternoon."

I noted that he did look weary. In youth, weariness manifests itself as a kind of burgeoning adulthood. The face and posture take on attitudes they are not used to assuming, a careworn air that still fits them ill, before becoming, through long usage, their natural state.

"I ask again: what was the service Thomas performed for you?"

"And I tell you again: I cannot say."

"But it was not to provide you with funds so you could marry Kate without my knowledge?"

"No."

"And you swear that she has not been compromised? Because, if so, a betrothal must be arranged for her right away, before it becomes obvious. I was trying to say as much to Thomas, but he refused to listen."

"Good God, was that your intention when you set off for Greenwillows in the first place? To insult our neighbor by offering to 'chip in' and buy his daughter a husband?"

"My intention was to save you."

"Save me from what?"

"From such temptations as are natural to cross the path of an innocent and foolish young man."

"Do you really despise Kate so much?"

"Despise her? My objection has nothing to do with her personal qualities."

"Really? Then what *has* it got to do with?"

"Her background, of course. The stock she comes from."

"Now who consults his Fancier's Handbook?"

"Alas, dear boy, therein lies the difference. The manual upon which I rely is Burke's Peerage."

"She has no title. What of it?"

"She has no *breeding*."

I saw I had at last broken through his air of supercilious reserve.

"If she has not enough breeding, perhaps I have too much. If I had less, I would hardly allow you to speak to me this way. I would hardly allow you to speak in such a fashion about the woman I . . . I . . ."

"Yes? About the woman you *what*?"

For a moment there was a silence as he honestly inventoried his own feelings towards the girl. Then we both became aware of approaching footsteps.

"Damn," I mouthed.

"As you see," Thomas crowed, "here he is, lying in state."

He showed me off as he would a newly purchased Shetland pony or some other barnyard curiosity. Kate, unable to restrain herself, rushed forward and threw her arms around me.

"Lying in state," I heard Seabold gently correct, over the girl's wrenching sobs, "is not really what one says about a man who is still—"

"Oh your Lordship! When I first heard I was beside myself!"

"There, there, child." I patted her distractedly, breathing in deeply, greedily, the scent of outdoors and wildflowers, of the world I had been, for several days now, deprived.

"We wanted to come right away but Doctor Rosewater warned—"

"It is all right, my dear."

"Are you going to die?" Jenny asked.

"Quiet child!" Mrs. Thomas shrieked.

"Indeed I am," I answered, relieved to have finally been asked the question. "But not today, it would appear. I am definitely closer, though. Certain outlines are being revealed."

"What is it like?"

She stood, as was only fitting, apart from the others, on tiptoe to gaze gravely over her sister's shoulder.

"Dying?"

Kate wailed and would not let go. Her mother came forward to attempt coaxing her off. I noted how Seabold, in front of her parents, did not assume the same degree of familiarity he did at the Hall.

"You must not listen," Thomas excused. "She has yet to learn the niceties of civilized conversation."

"It is like a house," I attempted to answer, speaking to the child alone, "in which all the partitions are being knocked down. The many rooms melt into one. And then, after a time, the floors go as well. But still I manage to move amongst them. Perhaps from habit. Indeed, I see for the first time how deeply ingrained habit is as a force of life, so much so that, even when all else slips away, one . . ."

That is all I recall, though there was more, of course. A distasteful scene, from what I gather, with the women weeping and Seabold frantically trying to mix a cupful of Rosewater's sleeping potion and pour it down my unwilling throat. There is, as I lie here again in that indeterminate time between night and day, the smell of opiate splashed around my neck and shoulders. Kate sleeps in the corner. Even in repose, worry is etched on her pretty face. I am puzzled by her seeming devotion. It appears the sole evidence I have ever been presented with for the existence of Divine Grace, the essence of which, as I understand it, is to be wholly undeserved.

April 25

Still here?

I am too, evidently.

You are frightened, aren't you? For if I die you will be left to face something dreadful. But what? Why do you not want to be alone?

What is it that makes you so afraid?

Have you sinned?

April 26

It all began with my going outside. The chamber pot was full and I could not bring myself to wake anyone by shouting. Besides, it gave me an invalid's sense of accomplishment to cast off the covers, pull on the new clothes Seabold had brought, and slip noiselessly out.

One associates spring with flowers and sun, birds building nests, a young man's fancy etc. etc., but surely the season is more truly typified by muddy earth, satiated with water and beginning now to firm, about to burst forth in a riot of growth. Not yet, though. At night, micturating while staring up at pale wisps of cloud and beyond them the pin-prick stars, breathing in the scent of a million vegetal assignations, I felt the promise, so much more poignant than the fact, of rejuvenation.

"The heavens are bright," I remember my tutor explaining. "Or so medieval scholars proved. Blindingly bright, with planets and moons moving like shimmering balls around the sun. A great celestial toy. Our modern vision of vast sterile distances between oases of spinning stone, signals, by contrast, a loss of faith, an inability or unwillingness to *see*."

There was barely a moon. Despite the poor man's ancient exhortations, my dark night of the soul was no mere phrase. I felt my way in what I thought was the right direction until my fingers met a rough-hewn piece of wood. No part of Greenwillows, where I had imagined myself heading. Yet I knew I had not walked far and tried picturing the various buildings within hailing distance of the house.

It was a door, that much was clear from how the wood responded to my touch. I remained outside, before the familiar rustle of straw told me I had gone as far as the stables, conveniently situated downwind from Thomas' soon-to-be-grand manor. The comforting smells of manure and liniment reassured my nostrils. I moved forward, holding the twin fragrances deep in my lungs as if they contained medicinal properties.

"And the dogs?" a voice asked.

"I gave them extra rations," another voice assured. "Besides, they know you."

"All the more reason for them to bark."

"You credit them with understanding?"

"No," she answered uncertainly.

There was a violent rearrangement directly before me, where I could have sworn a wall existed. It was then I had to admit my complete disorientation. The stables, yes, but the back of the building. I must have made a blind half-circuit, or stood so absolutely still that the earth itself had turned a fraction and forgotten to take me along.

"Stop," she whispered. "I told you, I only came to talk."

"That is what we are doing, is it not? Talking."

"I feel a presence. I feel someone watching."

"It is the beasts."

I was placed in an awkward position. It was apparent I had disturbed a swain and his lassie. To blunder about and reveal myself would lead to embarrassing discovery, while remaining still seemed almost to approve of what was taking place. I held my breath. The voices resumed.

"He says I've got to go," the man went on.

"I know."

"Some rubbish about 'too many hands.'"

"Yes."

"Too many hands, my eye! Everyone here knows I do the work of ten men."

This boast must have been underscored by a demonstration, for there was an audible slap followed by a deep chuckle at having elicited such a response.

"Says he'll give me wages," the voice went on, though the rest of him was still engaged in an unceasing assault. "Wages I haven't earned. Traveling money, he calls it. Travel where? I asked. He said, That's your lookout, lad."

"Stop!" the woman (whom I had realized with mounting horror was Kate) pleaded into the suddenly fetid air.

I fancied loose bits of straw were coiling themselves around my ankles, threatening to drag me down.

"Go back home, he says. Well what's at home for me but despair and misery? asks I. Then up north, he says. Or over the sea. Australia. Says he'll buy my passage. Why? I put it to you. Why is he doing this?"

"He tells me nothing," she whispered. "But if my father says it is time for you to go, then that is what you must do."

"And give up my prize?" he asked incredulously.

"It is no prize, what you speak of. More a mark of shame."

"That is not what you would have said a month ago. What has changed so much since, eh?"

You must act, I resolved. You must prevent what is taking place. Perhaps if you could divert his wrath onto your own person . . .

Edging forward, I held out my hands to feel for a loose piece of timber or stray implement.

"It has to do with that toff, I'll warrant. I have seen the way he looks at you."

"No," she objected, with fear in her voice. "Whatever makes you think so?"

"Whatever makes me think so?" he mocked. "Why, it is his place you spend all your time at now. That crumbling pile of bricks he calls a Hall. After he came here that day prancing on his great white charger."

"I told you, it was Father's idea, my going to Upton. I had nothing to do with it."

"And just this noon him and the Squire was talking. Eying me at the same time, they was. As if settling my fate."

"You are imagining things, Col. Why ever would they—?"

Cutting short her answer, he forced her slowly to the ground.

"You mustn't hurt him! You must leave him be! He has done nothing. He has been decent and kind."

"Oh I'll leave him be, all right."

"You must swear to it."

"I'll swear to it," he growled, "after you do some pretty swearing of your own."

I was poised to spring forward and hurl myself at the villain. But then there was a change, a tipping from one state to another. The balance between them shifted. Words were replaced by more primitive sounds. Both seemed in the grip of an unholy torment. It was not clear exactly what was happening, who was doing what to whom. All that *was* clear was how unnecessary, nay, how *wrong* my continued presence would be. The memory of Angela and Father, of my accidentally witnessing a similar encounter, clouded my vision. Defeated, I turned, letting the mutual concert of cries drown any noise I might make while shuffling out, as the two clawed their way to that most temporary of fulfillments.

"Close in there," I murmured, affecting nonchalance, mopping my brow, seeking solace in the crickets' refrain.

Internally, though, my mind reeled. Too much became clear all at once. Yes, Seabold had correctly perceived the threat to Kate's virtue, but seen too little or too late, considering how far things had gone. And now it became all too obvious what the "service" he had requested of Thomas was: to send Woodforde away. How had he phrased it, though, I wondered, so as not to implicate the man's own daughter? Simply that he did not care for

Woodforde's manner, for some insolent stare the hired hand had cast in his direction? And Thomas, what did he think? Doubtless that the Young Master was in the throes of love and subject to baseless fits of jealousy. I could imagine him at first pleading poverty, what with the sowing season coming, to lose such a steady worker, not to mention a relation of the wife, one of the family practically . . . all to enmesh the child even more fast in a web of complicity, playing up to the boy's naively chivalrous spirit. No wonder Seabold had tried raising funds to compensate Thomas, and, when that proved impossible, felt "duty-bound" to present him with the salver instead.

Sir Galahad indeed.

And what of Kate? Her tears at Upton, when I commended her innocent nature, when Seabold had called her "grand," when she realized what a flawless creature we both took her for, now became understandable. But where were those same fine sentiments when that barnyard Lothario first pressed his attentions?

Muffled groans penetrated the moist air. A solitary figure, perhaps roused by the continuing sounds, emerged from the house. At first it appeared to be nothing more than a small cloud billowing several feet off the ground, before the vision was translated to that of Jenny, her white nightdress flowing as she strode forward. I noticed how confidently she walked on her native soil. She had no need of a lantern.

"It was stuffy in my room," I explained, barring the way to the dreadful scene behind me. "I apologize if I woke you."

"I was going for a walk."

"A walk? At this hour?"

"Come."

She led me in the opposite direction, away from the buildings, guiding us past trees that magically stepped aside, along stone walls that gently funneled us towards an invisible goal. We proceeded in silence for some five minutes.

"Where are we going?"

"A place I know."

"Is it far?" I asked, for the path had grown steep.

"Here," she called, from further down.

Momentum dragged me the few remaining feet until I was able to stop myself inches short of inky water.

"The Tym," I exclaimed, recognizing the rush of current.

"I come here," Jenny said.

My eyes adjusted to what illumination shone off the glossy surface. I could see her small figure in relation to the towering trees and implacable river. Yes, there was no need for her to say more. She came here, as I once had, to gaze into its depths and try discovering what lay in wait.

"I must return to the Hall," I said. "I have put your family through too much as it is, imposing on your hospitality this way."

"We stayed with you. You stayed with us. Now we are quits."

"I suppose. Will not your parents, should they wake, be alarmed to find you missing?"

"They know I wander."

"Alone? At night?"

"You can see things more clearly at night."

"I would have thought the opposite."

"When the world is empty, you can see things as they truly are. It is people who confuse matters."

"Really? How so?"

"They get in the way."

The river lapped at its banks in eloquent assent.

"I have been thinking," she went on, "about that wizard."

"Merlin?"

"If he was living backwards, going from what would be to what had been, then what ever happened to him?"

"He dies, halfway through the tale. Or is buried, rather, under a lake. It is his absence, in fact, that signals the beginning of the chronicle's Time of Troubles."

"Troubles he already knew of," she pointed out.

"Yes. But not the bliss that preceded them."

"What was she like? Alice?"

I paused, though by now I should have been used to the sudden turns conversation with the young girl took.

"My wife, you mean," I corrected, stalling for time. "What was Alice like? She was a child."

The word came unannounced and hung there, radiating its full import. Was it true? I asked myself. Had I married a *child*?

"A young lady," I finally amended, "of good family, though recently orphaned. An uncle of mine, himself ancient, had been appointed her guardian. Sensing the approach of his own demise, he urged us to meet. In a flower garden. In Chelsea."

"Where is that?"

"A neighborhood in London," I explained. "There are houses, some with small gardens in back. This one had cyclamens and . . . snapdragons of many colors."

"Why did you wait so long?"

"To marry? I suppose I never felt the need. But then there was the matter of heirs to produce. And a certain loneliness to be assuaged. Also, it was expected of me. After my mother died, people began to talk."

"Talk about what?"

"They found my continuing to live alone . . . suspect."

She giggled.

I looked down and saw why. My stockinged feet, having advanced several steps, were ankle-deep in water. A darkness had climbed even higher, through the striped material of my hastily thrown-on trousers, to my knees almost, despite which I did not move back.

"She was waiting in the garden. I watched her before she became aware of me. There were bees hovering and one lit upon her hair. He made no distinction, I remember, between herself and a flower. She was a bloom among blooms. That is how I first saw her. Then and subsequently."

"Did she love you?"

"I do not know."

I never questioned her devotion at the time. But now . . . It was as if what I had just witnessed in the stable knocked all lies out of my head. Lies I had been telling myself for years. I could not say if Alice ever loved me.

"Did *you* love *her*?"

Again, a nagging doubt refused to let my lips form the easy response. Instead the silence lengthened. A ghastly retrospective light was cast over all that had gone before.

She picked up a stone and threw it in the water.

"I do not wish to love," she declared matter-of-factly, "or be loved."

Life, I realized at that moment, is what lies between Jenny and myself, which is why we are able to converse about it so dispassionately. Hers has yet to properly begin and mine, it became increasingly clear, as the ripples reached my sodden toes, is done.

April 27

A tolerable day, though chilly.

I am reinstalled here at Upton, after being mummified by all manner of blankets and cushions during the brief carriage ride home. When we arrived, Rosewater was waiting at the foot of the stairs to supervise my return.

"There is absolutely no need," I complained. "I am perfectly capable of walking."

"Purely a precaution, my Lord," he smiled, barely taking cognizance of my words, as I was borne on a kind of litter up to the second floor.

I fancied I saw, passing one of the more dreary hunting scenes hung on the landing, an obscenely grinning face visible only because I was flat on my back. The canvas, a Kilburne, was revealed to contain a sneering naked boy defecating into a bucket.

"Rum," I muttered, careful to evince no outward sign of surprise.

It feels good to be done; done with the misadventure of our curious houseguests; done too, I pray, with the corresponding madness that seemed to descend briefly on both Seabold and myself. I have never valued the solid, secure confines of the Hall more.

Despite the brevity of my trip, I must confess to a certain fatigue. I will rest before dressing for dinner. Seabold has ruled out absolutely my coming down, but I have a horror of being reduced to the invalid's tray and carafe of suspiciously weak wine. I will take him unawares, see what absurd creation he has cajoled Cook into producing. After the well-intended gruel served me at Thomas', there lurks in my belly an unusual hunger for the exotic.

April 28

. . . which I got in no small measure last night, though less by what was on my plate than in he who sat across from it. I woke to the gong, unsure if it was the first or second sounding, having passed the entire afternoon in deep slumber. Still groggy, I put on my dinner clothes, noting how much more loosely than before they hung on my once ample frame.

"—need to put some meat on my bones," I jauntily explained, breezing into the drawing room as if there was nothing untoward in my appearance.

Act normal, I counseled myself, rather than try and convince him of your fitness to remain. Treat your recovery as already accomplished. Do not look him straight in the eye.

Seabold, in turn, showed no surprise, despite the fact that my buttons met somewhat unevenly in front. Instead, he rose and, without asking, prepared us each a whiskey and soda.

There remained one task left me, a necessary albeit unpleasant one: to inform him of what I had seen at Greenwillows, and so put to rest once and for all any notions he may have had concerning the purity of Kate Thomas.

"I fear I have some rather distressing news for you," I began, sitting in my chair, proposing to tackle the awkward subject right away, without preamble.

"Do you?" he called, not turning.

"It concerns our mutual friend, for whom I have a great fondness. Almost as great as your own, though naturally of a different sort."

"Naturally."

He handed me my drink and sat back down. His own clothing, in contrast to mine, appeared to have been cleaned and freshly pressed. We held up our glasses in a silent toast.

Embarrassed, still unable to meet his gaze, I took a gulp and stared at the ceiling.

"It would appear your suspicions were correct. Her virtue was, as you put it, 'under assault.' I cannot credit how Thomas continues to shelter such a viper in the very bosom of his family. No doubt the man in question being a relation of his wife blinds him to the lout's essentially base nature."

"We are all blind to that which is close to us," he observed, with a hint of mockery I did not register at the time.

"Quite right. And your instinct to save the girl by having Woodforde sent away was admirable. I congratulate you on acting so decisively. But the thing of it is . . ."

"Yes?"

I found myself, at the crucial moment, quailing before the prospect of his disillusionment. Who was I to cause such pain and offer no solace in return? Yet you must, I argued, to ensure his future happiness, rocky as that immediate prospect might appear.

"It would seem the situation had advanced further than you thought. It would seem she has already . . ."

"Already what?"

I fixed my gaze more firmly on the cracking plaster, took a breath, and announced:

"It would appear she is no longer a—"

Another figure walked in. At first I thought it was Mann, or rather I assumed it was, and so did not bother to look. Not, that is to say, until he planted himself in front of me and stared in amazement.

"What are you doing here?" he demanded.

"I might well ask you the same question," I rallied, trying to cover my confusion.

For the young man filling my vision was remarkably similar in appearance to Seabold himself!

"Doctor Rosewater gave strict orders for your meals to be served in bed. I have just come from supervising the preparation of the tray."

"And what gives you the authority, a guest in this house, to 'supervise' anything?" I blustered. "Except your own deportment, an area in which, I must say, I find you deplorably lacking. Why, we have not even been introduced!"

I tried staring past him, to Seabold, appealing for support and enlightenment, only to discover that the personage I had been addressing as my grandson was clearly now someone quite other, of the same approximate age and so perhaps superficially similar in terms of sheer youth, sharing as well that uniformity dinner clothes confer, but with more prominent features, curlier hair, and a fixed look in his eye, not a twinkle but a dark glitter.

"It is my fault," he interjected, rising now to the full height a set of properly tailored trousers enables one to attain. "Your grandfather and I began to speak. Before I could say who I was we were quite deeply engaged upon a discussion of human nature. He spoke with such ease and assurance I did not realize until just now that he had mistaken me for yourself."

"I suppose I ought to be flattered," Seabold said dryly. "Grandfather, this is my good friend, Lucas Dalrymple."

"Not of the Ayrshire Dalrymples?" I asked, weak with confusion, making an abortive movement to rise but finding my haunches did not deem it worth the effort.

"I believe I have people in that part of the world, yes."

"Lucas claims he was summoned here. A wire I am purported to have sent, though I assured him I had neither the means nor opportunity. You wouldn't know anything about that, would you, Grandfather?"

"A wire?" I hemmed and hawed, quite sincerely at first. "Good gracious, no. Why, one can't send a wire from the village. One need go all the way to—"

"Hexham, yes. So I told him. Mann, apparently, had reason to go Hexham-way just last week."

"Did he now? Well, for candles, no doubt."

My face reddened as my mind, limping slowly, bringing up the rear, so to speak, reacquainted itself with the fevered mood it had been in just before I set off on my ill-fated journey to Greenwillows, recalling the search I made of Seabold's room, the intimate letters from which I culled a return address, and the subsequent composition of a telegram.

"Yes, I remember. Candles and sealing wax, I believe. But surely there has been some mistake."

"A happy one," the friend concluded. "I was knocking around Mayfair with no designs on the future whatsoever. The balls, you know, are in full swing, and I am not a dancer. My parents are doing their best to marry me off, but if one does not dance . . ." He fluttered his fingers. "Mandy's cryptic telegram could not have arrived at a more opportune time."

"Mandy?"

"A school name," Seabold said hastily.

I caught a glance exchanged between them, anger on Seabold's part, that of barely suppressed amusement on Dalrymple's.

"'A man's a man for a' that,'" he quoted Burns. "'A-man-da,' and so 'Mandy,' you see."

"Not really."

"Well," Seabold loudly cleared his throat, "that still does not answer the question of what you are doing down here instead of upstairs in bed."

"Being entertained by your delightful companion," I managed to answer, "and looking forward to a fit repast, if my nose is any judge of those odors climbing the back stairs."

"Then you insist on dining with us?"

"By all means."

"But the doctor said—"

"Bugger the doctor."

. . . if I do not have to stand in line, I added silently, glaring from one to the other.

"Very well. I shall tell Mann to lay another place."

He sighed, much put-upon, and left us once again alone.

An awkward silence ensued, which I attempted to break by asking, When did you arrive? Instead, however, I was horrified to hear issue forth from my lips the question:

"Are you a Sodomite?"

Caught in the act of downing his whiskey, Dalrymple could only raise his eyebrows in response, as if appreciating my frankness or perhaps debating, with a connoisseur's fine judgment, how to best answer such a discerning question. At last he set his glass down and replied:

"The 2:45. A tolerable train, until one leaves the coast."

"Yes. A bit slow, then. You were met?"

"I took the liberty of wiring ahead."

"Good. I am glad to hear it."

Was it my ears, then, and not my tongue, I could no longer trust? And what about my eyes, a moment earlier? They had betrayed me as well. Which sense would be next to go? Unless it was the unifying power behind the senses that had lost its bearings, in which case . . . who was "I" to even ask the question of myself?

"Any friend of Seabold's," I smiled, as the lad returned, "is welcome here. I must apologize for the earlier misunderstanding. As you may have been told, I suffered a fall several days ago and am not yet completely recovered."

"Your grandfather seems fine," Dalrymple reported. "Certainly not the stammering, doddering, knock-kneed, watery-eyed, incontinent old gent you described."

Now it was Seabold's turn to color. He did no such thing, however. He faced me without turning a hair and said:

"Cook is quite put out that you have made a hash of her plans. The tray was apparently on its way up when you—"

"A hash is precisely what I wished to evade by fleeing the premises. Not to mention one of her dreaded concoctions."

Perhaps you are merely perceiving the TRUTH, it occurred to me, after all these years, what the rest of the world, including yourself, has for so long sensed but refused to acknowledge, failed to act upon. Perhaps all youths are the same odious person, all friendships founded on perverse desire, all commonplaces masks for damning accusations.

Such a bracingly bleak view lent me courage. Making the effort, this time I was able to rise.

"Come, gentlemen." I swayed but caught myself and waved off their offers of support. "I have no need for pills or tonics this evening. Your youthful company is the only medicine I propose to avail myself of. Shall we go in?"

April 29

This, then, is my predicament: evidently it was not financial need alone that prompted Seabold's sudden appearance here at Upton, but a deeper, more profound distress of which I remained unaware. Now, through no fault of his own, he has been thrust back together with—who knows?—perhaps the very agent of grotesque entanglement that sent him fleeing here in the first place. And it is all my doing. Though really, I think a man of my time might be excused for assuming epistles signed with the flowery script of "Arabella" were penned by a young

Miss, not by a former coxswain, as he mentioned this morning at breakfast, of the Oxford Blues.

"Rowing is such a manly sport," he added. "It is a pity our friend here chose not to participate, despite my persistent encouragement."

"A bunch of hearties," Seabold sniffed.

"I thought it would be a way for you to conquer your fear."

"Fear of what?"

"Nothing, Grandfather."

"Why, of water."

"Who has a fear of water? Surely not Seabold."

". . . bordering on dread." He frowned at Seabold, puzzled. "I am surprised you went to such lengths to conceal it."

"No lengths," Seabold muttered. "If one does not live near the sea or a lake. the question simply never arises."

"But there is a river here, is there not? The Tym."

"Oh, the Tym," he dismissed.

I do not know which I was more upset by: the hidden fear, revealed, or the fact that, once again, I had been so completely unaware of such a strain in his character. What else do I not know about the boy? Or, more to the point, do I know anything at all about him?

"Why did you never mention this?"

"I thought it was apparent. After all, if one's father drowns, it naturally follows that—"

"It most certainly does not 'follow' naturally. Fears are given to us as challenges, as obstacles we are meant to overcome."

"In your scheme of things, Grandfather. Not in mine."

"You should have told me."

"Why? So you could taunt me with further evidence of my cowardice?"

"There is a boat here," I hazarded, "though it has not been used for many years."

"A rowing shell?" Dalrymple asked.

"More a dinghy-like thing with oars. Big enough for two. My sister and I used to take it out."

"If Great-Aunt Angela used it, that would make the craft ancient."

"I suppose. It was always stood up on blocks, though. And covered with a tarpaulin. Perhaps you could examine it. Find out if it is still seaworthy."

"A capital idea."

Seabold gave such a shudder I immediately regretted making the suggestion. His friend reached over and gave him a fortifying pat on the shoulder, though from the way the lad flinched it appeared to be more of a punch.

April 30

My aim in wiring "Arabella," in inviting "her" to the Hall, insofar as I can recall my state of mind at the time, was to provide an alternative to Kate, one whose more appropriate presence might underscore the impractical nature of whatever pastoral fantasy of shepherd and shepherdess Seabold was bent on entertaining. What an idiot I have been! Not to see certain facts which now appear as plain as the nose on my face.

Despite my ostensible recovery, I feel a great weariness, a sense of being continually tested by some mysterious and unknown Force.

Tested and found wanting.

May 1

I am in the garden, a shadow of its former glory but still heartening at this time of year. Neither Mother nor Father took particular pleasure in this place. Alice and I, by contrast, spent many happy hours here, but even that seems ancient history. We thought, at the time, we were taking it to some new height. Now I see our so-called improvements only hastened its decay. The modern varieties, with which we thought to revivify the vistas, have grown vulgar, oversized and ragged, taking over the territory of their more prim neighbors and neglecting, in a rapacious hunger for land, to flower as originally intended. Yet even the impending jungle has a certain charm. There are, just as one can poke through leaves and find unexpected troves of color, memories to be got here, previously undiscovered blossoms of long-ago incident rearing up out of the green, unsettlingly alive.

"How long have we got to wear these things?" I complained.

"A year, she says."

"A year! But at school they will make fun of me. Cathcart, when his brother died, only had to wear a bit of crepe."

"Be grateful you get to wear a uniform. I am black through and through. The dye has even stained my skin. Look!"

Concealed as we were on the floor of the gazebo, Angela had no hesitation in pulling down the front of her dress and displaying a line resembling a coal seam running just above her breast.

Mother's much vaunted disregard for convention did not extend to mourning, which she took with the utmost seriousness, forcing us to sport armbands, which even then were considered antique. In addition to clothing, all aspects of everyday life were made to take on a darker hue. Flowers were banned from the house, as was music. This former prohibition had the unintended effect of turning the garden into one of those childhood wonderlands packed with fantastic profusion and luxurious growth. Though in truth too old for such games, we both took a conscious step backwards, revisiting our days of innocent camaraderie with a youthful nostalgia which enabled us to escape, for a time, the unappetizing futures looming before us.

"Tell me the story about the ducks," I begged.

"Again?"

"It is different each time."

"It is not."

I rolled on my back. A flower, bulbous and purple and fuzzy, swayed over the ledge formed by the miniature sill as if spying, though there was nothing to see.

She spoke, once more telling me the tale and, as she did, eased off her shoe and through black stockings rubbed her foot. I watched, with great interest, her try to knead out some nervousness or fear through the very tips of her toes. But they were too securely encased. My gaze followed the line of her calf as far as was permitted, before the landscape plunged into night.

"He will come back, won't he?"

From the anxiety my voice betrayed it was clear I feared he would not.

"He said he would," she answered simply, although that implied, since Albemarle's actions often stood in opposition to his words, some degree of doubt, "after a decent interval."

"What will you do until then?"

"Console Mother. Stitch."

"Stitch?"

"She has set me to work learning embroidery."

The flower, responding to a breeze, dipped and beat gently against the wooden barrier above us. I reached up and plucked it, finding out only then, because of the thorns, that it was nothing more than an overgrown thistle, oddly puffed up, about to go to seed.

"You mean all you will do is wait?"

"It is a woman's lot."

"And what is mine?"

"To follow in Father's footsteps."

"What if I don't want to?"

The question seemed to puzzle her. She took the flower from me and fit it behind her ear. It burned defiantly against the black of her mourning.

"There is a boy from India at our school," I went on. "Prahmdinandi Major. We call him Swami. His father is a prince. Rich as Croesus, they say."

She lay down beside me.

"Last year, his father died. Swami didn't have to go to chapel after that. He was made to sit in the library instead. When we asked why, he said that, since assuming the throne, he had become an incarnation of the Brahma and so could no longer worship any other gods."

"But we are not heathens," she frowned. "And besides, you must protect me. You are the Man of the House, now."

May 2

The gentlemen, as Cook calls them, are out riding. I hope Seabold had the decency to assign his friend Fleur. I find it faintly disturbing to picture Episkidon's flanks being squeezed between the former coxswain's knees.

"Yet another guest," she exulted, summoned to my bed-chamber this morning. "It reminds me of olden times."

"What olden times? You were never here during Upton's heyday of entertaining."

"No. But I have heard tell. Receiving Dukes and Duch-esses. Hosting the Hunt Ball."

"Having Mr. Dalrymple here only means more work for you, I should think."

"Oh, I don't mind a bit of work. Besides, one extra mouth to feed doesn't require much effort, except for the special tisane he requests be prepared each morning."

"A special what?"

"Never mind, my Lord. It is your health we are dis-cussing. Doctor Rosewater gave me a list of what you can and cannot eat."

"A gentleman does not take a *tisane*, does he? Surely those are the province of maiden aunts and bachelor clergymen."

"He has the finest silk breeches, too," she confided. "Or so Mary says. He's got her doing his wash every day. She's clean gone on him, she is. But I shouldn't be telling tales."

"Indeed not. As for Rosewater's list, you may shred it into tiny pieces, boil it with dried flower petals, and serve it up to our delicate friend, for all I care."

"I would not say 'delicate,'" she objected. "Mary chanced upon him without his shirt. Apparently his torso fairly bulges with muscles. She said it was like a clay model she once saw of the Hebrides."

"Chanced upon him without his shirt *where*?"

"In the halls. He claimed he had lost his way."

It is Seabold who has lost his way, or so I wanted to retort, but held my tongue.

Has he, though? Does one have a "way," a predetermined path it is one's task to follow, to concentrate on, taking care not to stray, so that one does not even see the end, the ultimate goal, rising higher and higher, so fixed is one's gaze on the immediate?

The boy's relations with Kate come more clearly into focus now. Was he *willing* himself toward a type of normalcy? If so, one could hardly find a more attractive representative of the acceptable than she. At least on the surface. It would explain the extraordinary lengths he was prepared to go, substituting the noble gesture for more simple declarations he could not, in good faith, make.

And yet I saw in his attitude true affection as well.

The mystery of the human heart.

May 3

In the several days since his arrival, Dalrymple has made himself all too conspicuously "at home," giving no sign of when he intends to leave.

On another front, I have had a note in response to my thanking Thomas for his hospitality. It fairly rambles, as one would write to a longstanding friend, chatting of blessed events in the barnyard as well as the doings of each family member. All this in execrably "learnt" script, letters carefully traced out of a primer. I am being, no doubt, too hard on the man. Why his familiarity grates is a mystery. Father managed to be on practically backslapping terms with commoners of every stripe, maintaining an aristocratic dignity all the while, even when his brain was, a specialist once confided to Mother, "as shot through with holes as a piece of Antwerp lace."

One passage leaps out:

"Little Jennifer, our youngest, has been much affected by the departure of her cousin Colin. She has taken to sleeping where he did, in a cozy corner attached to the stabling facility, tending the beasts, helping them overcome their anxiety at his absence."

That is a fair sample of the man's atrocious style ("stabling facility" indeed!) but more importantly what I take from it is that Woodforde is gone at last. So Thomas has been true to his word, still thinking my grandson entranced by his daughter, little realizing she has been discovered to be nothing more than paramour to an overgrown stable boy, and—even more bizarrely—that a new and unexpected "suitor" has appeared.

What can I do, though? To answer in the same vein, to commiserate, i.e.: "My grandson and his friend spend their days exploring the district. The companion, who has a forceful personality and an almost mesmeric effect on the boy, openly debates whether or not to stay on here permanently, as if some compact has been arrived at requiring neither my nor Seabold's spoken consent," would be absurd. No, we are all, in our predicaments, fundamentally alone, more so as we age, as whatever hot life-force in us cools and our exterior, formerly a tide of molten lava which used to fuse with its surroundings or burn through obstacles in an accumulating headlong rush, hardens to impenetrable stone, incapable of changing shape save by being shattered.

May 4

Leaving the Hall for a walk this afternoon, I spied the two ambling off in another direction. Thinking themselves unobserved, they had the audacity to hold hands, or rather Dalrymple did, imprisoning Seabold's more reluctant grip in his own. Dangling from my grandson's other arm was an oddly-shaped canvas bag I had never seen before. I resolved to follow them, whether out of curiosity or because I thought to glean some relevant information I cannot say. Their path was sufficiently serpentine that I was able to stay well back, relying on snippets of conversation and trampled-down grass to show me the way. It ended at the boathouse. The river has shifted course since its construction, leaving the windowless box high and dry, as much on blocks as the craft it once sheltered. As I drew closer, I saw that the boat had been retrieved from storage and set out on a grassy plot of land directly before the doors, where the Tym itself used to eddy before taking itself capriciously away.

Dalrymple was, as the girl Mary had once chanced upon him, stripped to the waist, revealing not to my eyes a relief map of the Scottish Isles but certainly a well-developed physique. Freely perspiring, he bent over the gunwale to tar the inner seams. His taut musculature glistened in the sun. Seabold, not taking part in this act of nautical repair, had produced from his bag a sketchbook and what looked, from a distance, to be a lump of charcoal.

"Stop," he called, at a moment no discernibly different from any other in the latter's activity.

Dalrymple obediently froze in position, his back broadened, shoulders squared, quite the Adonis if one goes for that sort of thing, waiting patiently while Seabold commenced to draw his likeness.

"I feel my very soul being sucked out of my body," Dalrymple offered, after another minute.

"Why sucked out? Perhaps the opposite. Perhaps I am imbuing your body with the soul it previously lacked."

"I wouldn't know about that."

"A soulless creature would not, until it had been gifted with a soul's self-awareness."

"You are too deep for me, Mandy."

I was crouched behind a thick wall of reeds, having adopted that ignoble pose with no clear intent other than wishing to creep close enough to hear and not be seen. Luckily, each man's concentration was so focused on the other that my presence remained undetected.

"What did you do, then?" Dalrymple prompted.

"Must I resume this tale? It is a private matter. What concern is it of yours?"

"Your reluctance to tell makes it my concern. That, and the charming blush rising to the tips of your ears."

"If only the old man had not spoken out of turn."

"He merely referred to the situation in the most general terms. I am still unclear as to how it concluded. What did you do, after your last meeting?"

"What could I do?" Seabold shrugged. "We parted, the day Grandfather was well enough to travel. I accompanied him back to the Hall and found you here, along with your steamer trunk."

"And the milkmaid?"

"She is no milkmaid. I told you, she is the daughter of our neighbor. I have not had word from her since."

"Rather providential, then, my coming. Considering how deep in you were."

"Unlike you, I do not mind depth." Dissatisfied, he flipped to a new page in his sketchbook and began afresh. "It can be quite intriguing. The emotions it leads to. The thoughts of the future it breeds."

"Ah, the future," Dalrymple sighed, as if that too was something the very existence of which they disagreed upon. "So that is why I was summoned? Because you felt yourself menaced by the expectations of a milkmaid?"

"How many times must I say it? You were not summoned. At least not by me."

"'Come at once,'" he quoted, the words hammering themselves like individual nails into my conscience. "'I need you here. All is forgiven.' It was that last part that interested me particularly. That you would presume to forgive. For what, I wonder?"

92

"—some mutual friend playing a trick. Collins, perhaps. Though I would not credit him with the ingenuity of having the wire appear to come from Hexham."

"Forgive me for having brought you face-to-face with your true self? Is that the sin I must crave pardon for?"

"How do you know my true self is not the one who turned his back on all that?"

"Because the Mandy I know is not a coward. Or a fool. He knows he cannot flee what resides inside him."

"Don't be too sure."

"But I must. Be sure of you, that is, if I am to heap together all my sentiments like a pile of chips at Monte Carlo and push them forward onto a single number."

"You compare my favors to winning at roulette, Lucas? I had no idea I paid such high odds."

"The highest. Whereas to you, I sometimes feel I only represent a color (red or black, I cannot say which), a less individual, more cautious wager, one you see as promising less munificent a reward."

"Now who is too deep?"

"Tell me, if you had to decide between the milkmaid and myself, between the red and the black, as it were, whom would you choose?"

I found myself holding my breath. So Dalrymple had not told him yet. Why? Because he did not fully grasp what I was saying, or was on the verge of saying, that first night back, when I was at the height of my derangement?

Rather than answer, Seabold held up the page to gaze at his handiwork.

"May I move?"

"No. You have botched it pestering me with silly questions. I must try again."

"You seem quite taken with this Virgin of the Milking Station. More than I would have credited."

"I will thank you not to speak of her in that tone anymore. Now stay still."

"Very well," Dalrymple sighed. "I can deny you nothing."

It was the closest to a declaration of tenderness I had yet heard from the young man.

May 5

Sinned, how?

Thought I had forgot, did you? On the contrary, your presence grows increasingly oppressive.

Are you retracing the steps of your forefathers, searching out where the trail was lost, the wrong turn taken? What terrible deed has repelled you all this way, and how can I, a man who has many years since gone to face his judgment, help you evade your own?

It is the meddlesome tone of your interest that irritates. What is it to you if my father had unnatural relations with my sister? What business is it of yours, for that matter, if I myself engaged in certain disgustingly carnal games with Angela's fiancé? What right have you to know the intimate details of a family buried deep in the English countryside, details I have spent a lifetime expunging all evidence of, denying their very existence even to myself? Who *are* you, whispering persistently in my ear, doubting the veracity of the basic tenets I have endeavored to live my life by? What, I demand again, is *your* sin, yet to be committed, that condemns you to torture me in so subtle a manner?

Are you my descendants? All of you censoriously watching the events which led to your own creation? Which means Seabold must have married Kate after all, for otherwise our line is doomed to extinction.

Or he did not. And the place you watch from, journey from to perch on my shoulder with a flap of heavy wings, digging your remorseless talons deeper and deeper into my already pierced flesh, is that region where souls unborn glare out at their would-be progenitors for failing to conceive them. Is that the sin I must forestall: his failure to produce heirs? But it is not my fault! I did my bit. Against my better judgment, perhaps. God knows Alice would have been better off with someone nearer her own age and temperament, not a gloomy cantankerous man nearly three decades her senior. But prolong the line I did, just as I was expected to. As did Miranda, with a little forceful prodding. (There is a shameful act for which I shall never be absolved. Nor should I.) By God, we kept it going, did we not? By hook or by crook. Look at Mother and the extravagant lengths she went to, jeopardizing her very soul so that—

No. Ignore that.

It is time, I think, to put this book away. It has served whatever purpose it was originally intended for, and served it well. I was able to step outside my life, glimpse it whole, or whole enough. Enough to see it is nearly over and does not bear closer examination. The compulsion to record has become morbid, leading me places I do not wish to go. And so goodbye to you who, I see now, with clearer vision, do not in fact exist. Goodbye. Goodbye.

May 6

"Your Lordship's leg appears much improved," Rosewater noted this morning.

I refrained from telling him the alternate theory occurring to me: that it had grown worse. That the "mind of its own" my leg had been exhibiting, trembling, kicking, collapsing at certain moments, while haring off with a queer independent energy at others, had taken over my entire body, so that I was no longer responsible for my actions and could only tag along, supplying stammered excuses for what I had done or was about to do.

Instead, I directed his attention to the picture. We were on the stairs. I stopped, grasped his sleeve, and pointed out the boy squatting over the bucket, how the image was cunningly disguised in a clump of bushes tucked away in the corner.

"Such a mastery of craft," I lamented, "yoked to so tawdry an end."

"What else does your Lordship see?" the doctor asked, with seemingly genuine curiosity.

"Nothing . . . yet." I gazed at the expanse of cloud and tree, of receding landscape and expertly rendered horse-flesh. "Doubtless there are other concealed objects here and there, but I have yet to find them. It has not come together."

"Come together. To form a picture behind the picture, as it were?"

"No. A picture that *is* the picture. Both simultaneous and coincident with what it appears to be. The true picture, I suppose."

He appeared taken by this thought and stared with me for a time.

"It is a Kilburne, you say?"

"My father was quite fond of him, or rather called him 'the least intolerable artist,' because of the subject matter, I suppose, or what he perceived to be the subject matter. The hunt."

"You think, then, he never saw what you are just noting now?"

"It is possible," I conceded. "He was never much for contemplation, though. More a man of action."

At this point, Mary appeared at the doorway on the landing connecting to the servant's stair. She was taken aback at our presence, clutching, as she was, a load of freshly laundered linen.

"Excuse me, my Lord." She reddened, attempting to curtsey. "I didn't know—"

"Quite all right, Mary. Is that Mr. Dalrymple's wash?"

"Yes, my Lord."

"Has it done special, does he?"

"It is no trouble, my Lord."

We watched her hurry off.

"What do your people think of the love of one man for another?"

"My people?" Rosewater puzzled, as we resumed descending the stairs. "If you are referring to the children of Judah, my ancestors converted some three generations back. I could not train as a physician were I not—"

"Yes, yes, of course. But I imagine you are still somewhat conversant with your former faith, even if you no longer practice it in public. Able to pull a rabbi out of your hat, so to speak."

I frowned, wondering if that last bit had been spoken aloud.

"I believe all the great religions condemn such relations as unnatural."

"But are we not fundamentally 'natural' ourselves? We sprout, blossom, and die, just as the flower in the field. We gaze out on our plight with just as mournful an expression as the animal in the pasture, scamper ceaselessly to and fro much as any busy inhabitant of the forest. If we are not Nature, if what we do is not, simply by virtue of our doing it, 'natural,' then who are we and what is our purpose here?"

"We are created in God's image; and our purpose . . ."

Here the good doctor faltered.

"Yes?" I demanded impatiently.

"Your Lordship is perhaps more in need of spiritual, than medical, counseling."

"I want him to be happy."

We had arrived at the porte cochere in time to see Seabold and Dalrymple returning from yet another visit to the boathouse. Though displaying no outward signs of affection, there was a shared ease in their posture and gait that bespoke of more than mere exercise and its subsequent fatigue.

"One can bequeath many things," Rosewater opined. "I do not think happiness among them. Save by example, perhaps."

"Oh, my 'happiness,'" I scoffed.

He turned to me.

"If you value it so little yourself, how can you set such great store by it for your grandson?"

"One can wish happiness for others but not for one's own person."

"Really?"

"To reach for it is to push it away, as with a soap bubble. It dances just beyond one's fingertips. Or vanishes."

"Happiness then existing beyond our mortal reach, what remains to strive for?"

"I should have thought that obvious: adherence to a moral or ethical code, the satisfaction one gains from meeting one's obligations."

By now the young men were practically upon us.

"Nevertheless, I should think if your Lordship tried setting an *example* of happiness," Rosewater murmured judiciously, "that might be the best guide to Master Seabold's own pursuit of the matter."

May 7

On the eve of my departure, Mother summoned me to her dressing room, a boudoirish hideaway done in hanging silk so it admitted no direct light. My school uniform, contrasting with such overwhelmingly feminine decor, must have bordered on the comic, though at the time I was aware only of how the mirror, previously the altar at which she laid the daily sacrifice of her looks to age, was sheathed in a gauzy covering of black material, thus extinguishing her very existence as a desirable creature, ending a segment of her life forever. She lay on a chaise longue and motioned that I should take my place on a stiff-backed chair that did not belong to these surroundings. It had been, I recognized, dragged down from the maid's quarters, in the attic.

"What do you know of your sister?" she asked, once we had dispensed with a few pleasantries regarding train platforms and sandwiches.

"Know of her?"

"Her state of mind," she elaborated.

"She is well," I answered automatically. "She mourns, of course, but no more than is to be expected. Why?"

I was aware of being treated differently, of having my answers seriously considered.

"Your mourning, in contrast, seems to be of the more inward type."

I checked to make sure my armband was still in place, but also straightened my posture into an attitude of defiance. It was true, I cared not a scrap that Father had died and saw no reason to counterfeit emotions alien to me. Besides, her observation did not seem rooted in criticism, but approval, rather.

"She has taken up embroidery," I said, attempting to steer the conversation back to Angela.

"Yes. A woman does not even merit the luxury of having others nail her to the cross. She must crucify herself, stitch by stitch."

"I beg your pardon?"

"Her friend, the esteemed Lord Albemarle," Mother reached down and tore from her breast, as if it had been eating away at her, a letter, all while speaking in that casual way of hers, "has seen fit to cancel his visit."

"What reason does he give?"

"Grouse hunting in Scotland, though taking aim at more richly-endowed heiresses is no doubt closer to the truth."

"But why? I thought—"

"The details of our finances were made public as part of your investiture. Perhaps they were less than his family expected."

"No," I said, remembering my ill-timed burst of spleen regarding the others and their eccentricities. Doubtless that had cooled his ardor. Or was it my own refusal to act in concert, to declare myself as extravagantly as they had? Or was it something else?

Certain acts he proposed that I had balked at, more out of incredulity than disapproval, now suggested they were the cause for his having moved on.

She read over a few lines of the already much-perused notepapers and let them fall to the floor. I picked them up and goggled at the vapid yet elegant hand.

"Whatever reason he may have, he gives no clue."

"Not to you, but surely he has written her as well."

"No. Not a word to Angela. Nothing that could be construed as a promise and so nothing to be retracted. He is gone."

I felt a draining sensation. My heard jerked, just once, as if a hand, caught in mid-caress, had torn out some insignificant keepsake, a few wisps of hair, then took itself away.

"Have you told her?"

"That is your task now. It is why I called you in."

"Yes, of course. I shall attend to it."

I rose to go, then thought to take the chair I had been sitting on and lift it as well, so clearly was its presence only for the occasion of the rare male visitor.

"You remind me of him," she observed, as I shuffled awkwardly to the door.

"I remind you of whom? Father?"

"*Your* father."

Never had the careless way she spoke been more calculated. I walked a few more steps, before the penny dropped, as it were, then set the chair down.

"You will thank me some day," she went on.

I heard the rasp of a match striking and smelled, a moment later, the first whiff (so different, always, from those which followed) of tobacco.

"I saw too late, as I became better acquainted with your father's past, with his family history, the nature of the hereditary curse he bore. I saw too late to save Angela. But for you, William, my way was clear. Difficult, but clear."

"Was it?" I managed to ask.

"I tell you now so you will not be tortured by the thought you are doomed to follow his path. You are free of the demons which swarmed in his blood. There is none of him in you, despite what you may think, despite what others may tell you."

"Then whose—" I turned and confronted (if that is the word, for there was suddenly so much smoke in the confined space I could barely make her out) she who had matter-of-factly turned my life upside-down, "—whose demons instead take credit for my existence?"

"Ah, I was careful to have no answer for you there," she smiled, reclining into a pose of extreme self-satisfaction. "Of the three, I have sometimes played the private parlour game of trying to determine which lent some superficial prop, a stoop here, a stammer there, to your outward nature. But long ago I concluded that the confusion whirling inside me during that tumultuous time left you with no one Giver to call your own."

She stretched out further, almost invitingly.

"Except, of course, myself."

"But just now you said I reminded you of Father. Of my . . . real father."

"Of all three. It was when you said 'I shall attend to it.' I was reminded by certain domestic instincts you display."

"Domestic instincts?"

"Well, they were all necessarily of the servant class, William."

I picked up the chair again. I do not know why I was so determined to remove it from the room.

"I shall attend to—I shall tell Angela," I called numbly, over my shoulder.

My fears have come true. My hand is trembling just as my leg did, with just as disastrous results.

I manage to go back over what I have written and am appalled. What is this strange version of the past? Have I unseeingly dipped my pen in a different inkwell, one filled with a hideous witch's brew? Is this Madness Ascendant or its very opposite, a lifetime's worth of delusion falling exhaustedly away?

101

May 8

The next day, but I am scarcely recovered.

As much spectator as yourself to the latest revelation to come pouring from my pen, I see how, in the years that followed, I reacted strongly against what Mother told me, how I struggled to both ignore and refute the cold comfort she attempted to give me that day in her dressing room by becoming as much like Father as I could, aping the external manifestations of a character whose soul corresponded in no way to my own. I rode. I shot. I developed a streak of bluntness bordering on cruelty. More importantly, it was only after learning he was nothing to me, or rather that I was nothing to him, did I feel any true compassion for the man and at last began to grieve. If she thought the thunderbolt a release from whatever shadows threatened to drag me down, she soon had occasion to witness her fatal miscalculation, for it was legitimacy I craved above all else, if not a legitimacy of blood then of values held and actions taken. In those ways I would be his son. Otherwise, what was I? Cuckoo? Usurper? Or that other word, the one he used so freely, that, for the majority of my years, I could not even bring myself to say.

Was that why Father's delusions centered so on my unworthiness? For if my illegitimacy was not imagined, then all that followed made a kind of twisted sense. Perhaps it was the haunting suspicion that drove him mad, canted his mind to one side, tilted his view of the everyday world and freed, from underneath, all the subterranean goblins that lay in wait.

Thus, in one sense, my behavior in the years that followed was an elaborate charade, but in another . . . Is it not by the clumsy process of imitation that most of us construct our mature selves?

Perhaps, though, Mother knew exactly what she was doing, for in rendering me a poor copy of he who had gone before, she effectively maintained her own position as sole sovereign of the Hall. Alas, Time had other tricks up its sleeve. But of those she knew nothing, yet.

May 9

Either my condition has improved or the recent fair weather to some extent compensates for my disabilities. No longer muddy, not yet baked, the soft ground receives my footsteps as if welcoming an old friend. I still require a stick, but the weakness in my side has somewhat abated. More importantly, I feel a renewed eagerness to go out, to escape the ferocious introspection of the past few days.

May 10

I returned from the above-mentioned constitutional to find a familiar dogcart once again standing idly before the Hall.

What on earth? I wondered.

There were, I heard now, voices coming from the drawing room, those of young people laughing. The "gentlemen" had brought back from their excursion the "ladies" of Greenwillows. It gave me a strange melancholy to know I must go join the impromptu party, tainting their unadulterated pleasure with a reminder of age and decrepitude. And so I lingered a moment longer.

How is it we are able to sense ourselves being watched? The eyes emit no rays, there are sounds aplenty outdoors, yet gradually I became convinced that a person was observing me from behind the boxwood hedge lining the drive.

Of course, I recall thinking: the boy with the bucket.

It in no way invalidated my certainty that the lad existed only in a painting, if, indeed, even there. I have come, since my accident, to be more aware of the spirit-world through which we move, to the extent that I pity those who remain blind to it, as one would pity a man seen too far off to warn of a hole he is about to step into. What "the boy with the bucket" meant, whether a real, malevolently leering scamp or a treacherous oily spot in the morality of things, a slippery invitation to sin, was immaterial. "He" existed, in my mind, as much as Upton itself or the snatches of gay revelry I made out floating through the open window. A slight rustle from the confines beyond the drive only confirmed what I knew for a fact *to be*.

Nevertheless, I made no sign, far too cunning a dog for that. When the observer remains confident he is undetected then he, in turn, becomes the observed! Instead, I made as if to enter the Hall and slipped sideways, just beyond the door, to pad with exaggerated speed down a passageway leading to the loggia and from there out back, through the garden, and around. On the way, I seem to recall passing Mann balancing a tray, but, having no time to lose, affected not to see him and he, a skilled manservant, proceeded without a murmur of recognition, though at one point we were less than six inches apart.

It is possible I am becoming invisible, I mused, emerging behind the carriage house, which would give me a clear view of the drive and crescent.

To stifle the panting breaths this unexpected bout of activity had left me with, I paused a moment, leaning against the bricks. The Hall had a cockeyed grandeur to it, late sun investing its flaws with magnificence, as if they were the true state to which all things aspired, the shabby, the ramshackle, the disrepaired asserting themselves in evening to claim their rightful place. Mastering my pounding heart, I poked my head round the corner and was gratified to see a figure crouched just where I thought he would be, on the other side of the hedge, his face almost buried in the branches. He was trying to part them, to see further, no doubt, and get some sense of the goings-on within.

"You are always spying on people, Billy," I heard Mother's voice reprimand. "Sneaking about. It is undignified."

"Rather," I answered across the ages, "it is people who insist on presenting their unguarded selves. If one remains alert, everyone, simply by going about his or her daily business, appears shockingly exposed, caught in some act. Should I avert my prying eyes? Wear a bell around my neck to warn them of my approach? Besides, this chap here hardly deserves your protection. Look! He is far more indecently peeping than I have ever done."

Nevertheless, seeing such a broadly-drawn caricature of my own proclivities did make me frown in shame. Only for an instant, though, because he then reached into his shirt and drew out what glittered in the slanting sun as unmistakably a knife. I started nearly out of my skin, imagining some horrible act of violence, before I saw— with first relief, then outrage—that he was meticulously cutting away at the shrubbery.

"See here!" I barked, forgetting completely to what lengths I had gone to conceal my person. A bit of green wall snapped and, with it, a corresponding branch of my soul fell to the ground. "Stop that at once!"

I strode forward, boots crunching on the gravel drive. Startled, the man looked back. Not a boy at all, but fully grown, with a face marked heavily by its primate ancestors. (I have read and, insofar as I was able to follow his argument, am in full agreement with Mr. Darwin, so long as one keeps in mind that the "evolution" he speaks of is in response to a world *created by God*. Indeed, how could a man, were he merely a lump of protoplasm, conceive such a grand theory as the above-mentioned gentleman has posited? No, his very energetic attempt to stamp it out proves beyond all doubt the existence of a Divine Spark.) Knife still in hand, the stranger squared his shoulders, readying to repel a coming assault. All I did, however, was place myself a few yards off and demand:

"Who are you, sir, to come here and destroy property?"

With sullen deliberation he put the blade back in his belt and began moving off. I noted common clothes, worse for the wear, as if their owner had been sleeping under the stars or, more likely, in a ditch, and sure animal movements. A true son of the soil. Only his eyes, with a puzzled squint to them, betrayed any hint of unease.

"Wait," I called. "I am not through with you yet. Where do you come from?"

But he was determined not to speak. It was akin to coming upon a solitary wolf who grudgingly retreats without giving any sign of fear or hurry. Just then, from the open window came a peal of laughter, instantly recognizable in its purity and delight—Kate, the essence of her—causing him to stumble in his retreat and turn for an instant, his face contorting with rage.

"Curse her!"

I followed his gaze beyond the hedge to an all-too-easily-imagined scene of ease and privilege, then returned my attention and found him gone, though there was no obvious direction he could have taken. The earth had swallowed him up.

Sagging a bit (it was only then I realized the extraordinary rate at which my blood had been pounding), I went over and searched for the fallen branch. I do not know what I intended. To fit it back into the rigid company of its comrades? By morning it would be brown and lifeless. In any event, there was no evidence of whatever damage he might have done. It was, I realized vaguely, an employment for my external senses, so my mind, working at full speed, could continue trying to solve the problem it had been presented with.

Curse her.

The words, as they took their place in my memory, fit with those I had heard before. Once again I listened to the thrashing of straw as bodies met, to the mutter of sinners caught fast in chains of lust. Col Woodforde's face, seen clearly now for the first time, matched all too well the intimate acquaintance I had previously made with his voice alone.

May 11

A week ago, I resolved to write in this book no more. But I see such a vow has had no effect on my practice.

The truth is, I feel a growing superstition that so long as the nib of my pen scratches reassuringly over the surface of these pages, I will not be taken, my heart will not be torn from my chest and weighed against . . . what was it the deities of the ancient Egyptians used to ascertain that organ's purity? A single feather.

From what fabulous bird?

I had supposed Woodforde gone, indeed Thomas' chatty missive said as much. Clearly he is no longer at Greenwillows. Where, then? A man cannot hide in this district very long without someone taking note, nor can he feed himself, save by theft or poaching.

The more I meditate on it, the more I am convinced he is the roving malignant embodiment of that which must be fought.

For so long, I lived as if such a force did not exist. Pure Evil was reserved for the Garden and the Afterworld. Life took place in the vast variegated plain between the two. But now, as that once fertile valley narrows to a strip of land I can barely plant my feet on, I find myself encountering beasts out of a forgotten fairytale, save that, unlike the fire-breathing monsters of my infancy, these current creatures all too conspicuously lack the element of make-believe. They are real. They walk the earth.

May 12

The boy refuses to yield up his mystery. I have taken to studying the painting each day, pausing on my way downstairs, hoping the vision will have either melted back into the simple illustration whence it came, or grown more fully coherent, become not just an isolated figure, but one element in the hidden scene he first suggested by posing as such a tantalizing clue. Alas, neither development has taken place. Instead he remains as before, taunting me with his naked backside, head twisted so his eyes seek out my own.

This morning, I was once again trying to solve the mystery when Dalrymple emerged from the hidden door.

"Lost your way?" I echoed ironically, recalling his excuse to Mary.

At least this time he was properly attired, clothed in a snowy white shirt and trousers belted absurdly high, to the ribs almost.

"Found, more like," he answered without a trace of embarrassment. "My way, that is. There are so many passages and half-stairs. One is presented with a veritable warren of choices."

"All leading to the same end."

"I suppose. But there is the journey to consider, as well. Your Lordship fancies the art of the hunt?"

"Not particularly."

"I do. This is an intriguing example. What would you say is depicted?"

"It is clear enough. They have run the fox to ground. The dogs, you see, are worrying him out of his hole. About to tear him to pieces."

"Yes, but . . . note in the corner. Is it possible they have been detained by a false scent?"

"How so?"

"Don't you see? There! I believe our quarry is escaping."

It did appear to be the tail of a fox disappearing over a rill in the extreme distance, bounding into the ornate tracery of the frame itself.

"How long," Dalrymple mused, "before they realize their error? Too late, I fear. You see the sun is already high. He has lived to fight another day."

"But the painter has caught him," I pointed out. "Grabbed him by the tail, as it were."

"Yes, I see your Lordship's point. He has escaped their attention, but not our own. What will we do with him? Our prize?"

"I worry about my grandson, Mr. Dalrymple."

"I must confess I do as well. Everyone worries about Mandy. Perhaps it is an attitude he cultivates."

"I worry about what sort of life he will have."

"More of the same, I would imagine. Is that not really the only 'choice' we are offered?"

"No," I said firmly, "though it may appear so at your age."

"You think him at a crossroads, then, but with his head hung so low or stuck so high he does not perceive it as such?"

"Precisely."

"The same might be said for any of us, at any time in our lives, might it not?"

"You, I sense, know exactly where you are going."

"Do I? But even if that were true, it makes me no more qualified to guide my friend in whatever decisions he must confront. Is your Lordship coming down?"

"In a moment. Will you be seeing the young ladies from Greenwillows again?"

"As a matter of fact, yes. We ride there this afternoon."

"Have you told him yet?"

"Told him?"

"What I so rashly divulged that first evening, when my senses were still so jangled from having been transported home."

"I am not sure what your Lordship is referring to."

"Ah, well then . . ."

"Do you mean about the milkmaid being a more country sort than he imagined? That her innocence has been sullied by a brush with . . . well it sounded like the most base sort of mischief, from the way you shuddered."

"Yes. That's it."

"No. Of course I haven't told Seabold. Why should I?"

"Why should you not? It would strengthen your cause."

"By taking advantage of an elderly gentleman's indiscretion? By betraying an unintended confidence? I do not see how placing myself in such an unflattering light could do my 'cause,' as you put it, much good."

Facing forward, standing side by side, our hands gripping the railing, I was reminded of two supplicants, strangers united only in worship, that invisible but surprisingly tough bond.

"You yourself do not know what is best for him." I worked it out. "That is why you encouraged his once more inviting the girls here. So you could meet Kate. Meet her and then perhaps come to some decision."

"Which morsel to best break my fast on is, at the moment, the only decision I am capable of entertaining. Your cook has a particularly deft hand with eggs."

"One more question," I ventured to ask. "Do you notice anything unusual about these bushes?"

About to turn, he gave a last careless glance at the area I pointed to.

"They are awkwardly done. A late addition? Painting out an unwanted figure? More likely the work of an apprentice. I believe Kilburne was known to employ assistants."

I waited for him to proceed, then reached out and softly ran my fingertips over the paint. Its surface, barely disturbed, save by the occasional duster, since the time of its inception, was smooth, the fog of a breath on a windowpane.

May 13

So he has not told.

I listen again to the conversation I overheard at Greenwillows, to the fear and unwillingness in her voice, and begin to develop a growing understanding of the trap into which the poor girl had fallen; even, dare I say it, a sympathy? Perhaps she is not so irretrievable. Yes, there was sin, but inadvertent. Besides, it is how one acts after, how one picks one's self up, dusts one's self off and proceeds, that is the true test of character.

Could Seabold, I wonder, be happy with such a person, one who speaks to the yearnings of his sensibilities but not, perhaps, to the deeper pull of his nature?

What, on the other hand, would such a union be like for her?

And who am I, of all people, to presume knowledge of what is best for either?

May 14

Once launched, we felt beyond the reach of everyday society. I do not mean that we engaged in practices so awful, just that we were freed from invisible constraints. Outwardly, we remained simply a brother and sister in a small craft. I took a young man's delight in testing my newfound strength, pulling us miles up the current so we could drift back down. There was a small carpentered box built into the hull where Angela stored her "treasures," as she dubbed the simple fare she smuggled aboard.

"It is called Tokay," she explained, producing from its plain burlap covering a bottle of amber-hued liquid. "They say the Hapsburg Emperor drinks nothing else."

"Does Mother know you took it?"

"Mother never goes to the cellar."

"Then how did you get the key?"

She did not answer, but produced two glasses, set them on the box's wooden top, which served as a table, and looked to me expectantly.

"Well?"

"Well what?"

Neither of us, it transpired, had ever used a corkscrew. There ensued a scene of much hilarity, too long repressed by the unrelenting gloom at home, as together we mastered the complicated device and drew the stopper out. The wine (I blush to think what spectacular vintage we gulped as if it were so much ginger beer) heightened a sense of unspecified celebration.

She lectured in a consciously schoolmasterish tone.

"The grapes are affected by a type of fungus called 'noble rot.'"

"Who told you such things? Surely not Father."

"No. Not Father."

"It makes my head spin."

"We *are* spinning, silly." She motioned to the prow of the boat, which was pointing now downstream, now towards shore.

"Well who, then? Was it him?"

"No. Not him either."

We never mentioned Albemarle by name. More than a year had passed but, after my initial halting announcement of his cancelled visit, all mention of the subject was scrupulously avoided. Which did not mean that he was thought of any less. Rather, we imitated the ancient Israelites, refusing to write out even the letters of our God.

"It was Steele who told me."

"Steele!"

She measured herself another glass.

"You are shocked I have conversations with a man-servant?"

"No." I was, but endeavored not to show it. "Of course not."

"*He* is. Steele, I mean. He gets a look on his face when I ask him things."

"What kind of a look?"

She sipped her wine.

"Like the look you have now."

I laughed awkwardly and reached for the oars. She caught my glass before it fell.

"Noble rot," I jested, trying to recapture some of the giddiness we had felt just a moment earlier.

"See what else I have."

She reached down into the box and took out what I first supposed to be a piece of jewelry, though of an extraordinarily large and thick variety, fit more for a giant than her own delicate wrist. It was a bracelet, with no ornamentation, just a simple circle, lovingly burnished, the surface worn from use except where one link of chain hung.

"It is Father's," she explained, seeing my puzzlement. "From his room. When Mother had it taken apart I salvaged this."

"You took one of his shackles?"

"Rodgers said they were the only thing that kept him here, remember? That without his chains Father would float away completely. He never said that to you?"

"Certainly not. We barely spoke, Rodgers and I."

"We did, on many occasions."

"You seem to have developed a streak of familiarity with the help," I muttered, surprising even myself with my priggish tone.

"You are always away. And Mother shuts herself up. Would you like it better if I spoke to the walls?"

I hefted the ring of much-battered steel in my hand. The single remaining link clinked against its side.

"I sleep with it," she said, and then, seeing my look of consternation, added, "Some day you, too, William, will have a daughter."

"Yes, well, what if I do?"

"Then you will understand."

May 15

Not, of course, that I committed any sin so gross as his. I must be careful here. I see, as I delve unwillingly deeper into this cave of remembrance, that the shadows cast by my torch are bizarrely distended exaggerations, truth made out through the thick gloom of all the years that followed. Mother was no more the unfeeling creature I portray than I am doubtless perceived as being of a similarly cold nature by Seabold . . . into whose bedchamber I barged at two o'clock this morning.

"What do you mean 'She speaks to me?' " I demanded.

"Grandpapa?" he queried in a tone of disbelief, grinding balled-up fists against his eyes.

I was touched by his falling back on that name, what he used to call me as a child.

"Your mother," I elaborated, clearing a space on a chair, letting a pile of papers cascade to the carpet. "You said your mother 'speaks' to you."

"Did I? When?"

"Some time back. When the girls were first with us, I believe. Their recent visit must have jogged my memory."

He had by now sat up. I was disconcerted to see he did not wear a nightshirt.

"What's that?"

"What's what?"

"On your chest. Were you in some kind of altercation?"

"It is nothing," he said, hastily pulling up the covers. "As for Mother, I sometimes turn to her, that is what I doubtless meant."

"Turn to her?"

"Rely on her for advice or consolation. Pour out my troubles to her memory. Surely that is not so odd an impulse."

"Odd enough. She is dead, Seabold. And of memories you have none, save what I was able to provide."

"No memories of *yours*," he replied sharply. "You were chary enough with your reminiscences, and the ones you did let escape inevitably ended on a cautionary note, as if she were some bad seed I should take care not to emulate."

"I was trying to raise a child."

"More fend one off, was the impression I received."

"Are they bite marks? Have you let Mrs. Ellis cleanse them with carbolic soap?"

"Grandfather, I cannot tolerate these intrusions!" he shouted.

We waited to see if his outburst had roused any kindred spirits elsewhere in the Hall. When it became clear it had not, he continued in a more quiet, determined tone:

"She speaks to me, yes. And always has."

"What does she say?"

"What I want her to, no doubt. I am not fool enough to think her soul is actually communicating with me from

Heaven. She advises. Scolds sometimes, when she thinks I am in error. You may call her my conscience, if you must. And yet there are times when she . . ."

"When she what?"

". . . when she seems gifted with insights I could not possibly have arrived at on my own. Or when she forecasts events no one else could predict."

"Did she predict your meeting Mr. Dalrymple?"

"I am not prepared to discuss—"

"I wonder, Seabold, why your friend stays on here. Has he no position to fill back in London? Is he of independent means? Does not his family expect him home anytime soon?"

"No, no, and no, in answer to your questions. As for why he stays, he professes himself quite taken by the countryside. Surely you can sympathize with that. You are always urging me to appreciate it more. He even speaks of settling down here."

"Settling down and doing what?"

"Well, what is it you do, Grandfather?"

"Uphold a tradition," I answered stiffly, "not violate biblical injunctions, drive the staff to distraction with demands, and walk the halls half-naked, from what I am told."

"I expect he would answer he upholds a tradition as well, of a different sort but no less ancient."

"Yes, one of unbridled sensuality. It is from his upholding such a 'tradition' that you got those bite marks, I'll warrant. I do not understand how you have fallen under the sway of such an impudent, swaggering—"

Rather than resort to speech, he stilled my complaint with a look.

"If you crave memories," I grudgingly allowed, "that, just then, was the essence of your mother, practically undiluted."

"What was?"

"That killing glance. She could stop me dead in my tracks when she stared at me so. You have inherited the same gift, though you do not employ it as often."

"You give me less cause."

"I loved your mother, as I loved no one else."

"To her misfortune."

"Is that what she tells you?"

He turned away, lying on his side and trying to sleep.

"Of course you are right, Grandfather," he yawned. "How could she possibly speak to me when I never heard her voice? It is to you she must speak, but you have turned a deaf ear to her all these years, not to mention previously, when she was alive, when you turned a blind eye as well, I am told."

"Told by whom?" I grasped wildly at what seemed a clue. "Who has been telling you things, if not her shade? What does she say, Seabold? Tell me!"

I waited for a response but his breaths only grew more deep and regular. He had slipped, with no visible sign, from wakefulness to slumber.

May 16

To be more clear: I did not repeat Father's awful desecration of his daughter's innocence. What I did (so characteristically, I see now) was flee, travel too far in the opposing direction, maintaining a dignity towards her person that could all too easily be mistaken for indifference. It was nothing of the sort, of course. It was fear; a fear of kindling the same conflagration that, I came to realize, had engulfed he and Angela both.

May 17

Another cloudless day. Colors have appeared where there were none before, as if the habit of flowering had spread to mere objects. Fences, piles of stones, a derelict coach, all sport hues of amazing intensity. People, too, have been coaxed open by the light, bathing their faces in it, shedding the heavy garments that threatened to become additional layers of skin during the interminable winter and its harsh cousin, early spring. It is another season now, one not to be found on the calendar but felt by all.

The gentlemen's affinity for the misses of Green-willows has blossomed as well. The four meet almost every day at one or the other's establishment. I confess not knowing what to make of it all, though the presence of Dalrymple, paradoxically, lends a more innocent air to the proceedings. Under his direction, they engage in the time-honored activities of the young: music, parlour games, gentle sport. Today they have organized a picnic. Kate and Jenny's family, in its entirety, is to be there, and though I do not relish another dose of Thomas' conniving sycophancy, I have been persuaded to attend as well.

Cook, predictably, is in a frenzy of preparation, though she managed to find time to send word that I please not toss aside the extra blanket she ordered packed.

"For it gets quite cold in the afternoon," Mary, the bearer of these tidings, just recited, "and his Lordship tends to underestimate."

"Underestimate what?"

She looked at me, puzzled.

"That is all she said, my Lord."

"I tend to underestimate."

"Yes, my Lord."

"Underestimate the fullness of the spring? The strength of my recovery? The amount of common sense a gentleman requires to eat a meal out-of-doors?"

"I wouldn't know, my Lord."

"Ask Cook how she dares presume to—?"

I paused. Even the thrill of doing battle via such a conduit as Mary and her solemn approximations is not worth an hour better spent admiring God's glorious handiwork. If I think of it, I shall bring back a flower to press in this book.

117

May 18

It started innocently enough. But then it always does. Innocence is only recognized as such when seen in relation to what follows.

Despite or perhaps because of Cook's objections, I elected to walk, entering the wood and proceeding along the gentle rise some three-quarters of a mile until the trees began to thin and the sun grew hot. Laurie's Knob is, in all honesty, not so great a climb. A barren, rocky patch, it spans our twin estates, though because of its worthlessness no wall or marker has ever been erected.

When I arrived, the others were already in evidence, having set out a large cloth on which various platters and baskets were arranged. It was a charming scene, made even more picturesque by their initial obliviousness, none expecting me to emerge from the wild directly behind them. Mrs. Thomas attended to the needs of the little ones, five or six in all, if you counted a squalling bundle. Kate and Jenny were entertained by the young men. Thomas, pacing nervously, kept a close eye on the road that wound up the other side of the mountain.

. . . anticipating my arrival, I realized.

"He dressed himself up as a gypsy," Dalrymple was recounting, "and with me under his skirts, so when he opened his mouth to speak, it was my voice that came out."

There was admiring laughter at this subterfuge.

"And what kind of fortunes did you tell?" Kate asked.

"Why, truthful ones, of course," Seabold replied. "If they were not true when we made them, we made every effort to ensure they became true, in time."

"These were fellow members of our college," Dalrymple explained. "It is easy to tell a boy's fortune. Indeed hard not to."

"Could you tell mine?"

"Ah, girls are another matter."

The youngest member of the group muttered something.

"What's that, Jenny?"

"Girls," she enunciated more clearly, "don't have one."

"Don't have one what?"

"A fortune to tell."

"How so not? I would have thought that is all they have."

"She is quite right," I announced, once again experiencing the uncomfortable sensation that I had grown invisible. "A girl's fortune is to become a woman, so inevitable a process it hardly requires a crystal ball (or two jackanapes crowding into one piece of clothing) to predict. Whereas a boy," I fixed a rather dubious gaze on the two youths, "may remain a boy practically forever."

"Your Lordship walked?" Thomas staggered as he turned, twisting his neck this way and that, expecting to find a glass-walled coach hidden behind a boulder.

"I wished to earn my supper," I said, admiring the view.

Episkidon and Fleur, along with various conveyances, stood in a small patch of shade some several hundred feet below. Beyond them, the countryside stretched away, the Tym not visible but clearly marked by willows and other vegetation it had gathered to its banks. In the distance, a small puff of smoke rose. Hawks, their wings taut, balanced motionlessly on unseen currents. All around us were ancient rocks.

Thomas bustled over to the hampers and corked bottles while I remained immobile, staring into the distance, though there was nothing so singular to see, save distance itself, as if from this height it were tangible, a physical property existing along with fields, river, and sun.

". . . cold beefsteak, ham, a wheel of Green Wenslydale."

"I would have ordered my last case of Côte Rôtie sent," I answered, still entranced, "had I known."

"Oh, there is no need for that. Your cook mixed up a vast quantity of lemonade."

My attention was brought from far things to near by the presence of the ubiquitous salver, set off to one side of the makeshift buffet. Nothing was set on it, so it resembled a mirror reflecting the flash of emptiness overhead.

"Ah, you noticed," Thomas said appreciatively, having piled a nauseating mass of victuals onto my plate. "Won't your Lordship sit?"

"I cannot. Or rather I can, but then I cannot get back up again."

"Never really wanted it," he confided in a lower voice, following my gaze to the serving tray. "Master Seabold gave it as a token of his appreciation when we put him up those few nights. We was just being neighborly, I tried to explain. But he insisted. I imagine he did not know its true worth. Then I saw you eying it, when you graced us with your presence. Clearly your Lordship has a shrewd eye for value. So today I included it with our other vessels, hoping . . ."

"You are endeavoring to return it."

"Quite so, my Lord. But the lad will have none of it. I thought perhaps you could speak for him?"

"The item is his," I answered, refusing to fall in with the man's conspiratorial tone, "having descended to him through his mother. He may choose to dispose of it as he wishes."

"Speaking of inheritances," he went on, drawing me off from the main party, "we never had a chance to resume our talk about the future and what it may hold for those who come after us."

"The future?" I felt a familiar fire return, akin to what an ancient cavalry mount must sense when once more summoned to battle. "My grandson is not in the direct male line. The succession is subject to the law of primogeniture. There being an absence of any collateral branch—cousin, bastard, imposter or whatnot—the title will go extinct upon my passing, though he can, of course, petition the Court Herald and, through that office, Her Majesty."

"This time you do speak of Master Seabold," he tried assuring himself.

"Quite. Seabold the Penniless, as he could then be granted charter to proclaim himself. So of 'the future,' as you put it, regarding Seabold and your daughter, there is none."

"Your Lordship misunderstands. I had no intention of proposing—"

"Of course not! You wish for Kate a match that will leave her the happy mistress of a thriving home, not companion to a wandering minstrel singing for his supper at the estates of various school chums while vainly attempting to conceal the holes in his shoes, not to mention those in the footwear of his unfortunate mate."

"Oh, no daughter of mine will ever go begging," he observed, raising a cup of lemonade to his lips.

There it was, then. Would snaring Seabold, even without the title, be such a prize that Thomas was willing to settle on the girl a significant portion of his own wealth? Or perhaps he knew I was bluffing, that the title, though technically challengeable, could, if pursued through proper channels, most certainly be passed down. The overarching question was *how much*? I felt like an old trout, survivor of many a battle, staring warily at yet another temptingly baited hook.

The sound of musical notes made us turn. Dalrymple, ever a surprise, had brought with him a small harmonium, which now sat at the edge of the only remotely flat patch of ground. We watched him with unexpected talent draw lively music from the wobbling box, while Seabold instructed Kate in what he swore were the latest dances. Our forming an impromptu circle gave me the opportunity to edge away from Thomas and stand next to Jenny.

"I hear you have new lodgings," I murmured, using the twin diversions of music and laughter to mask our exchange. "Those formerly occupied by your cousin."

She turned, just for a moment, before deducing the source of my information.

"The beasts missed him," she replied, again staring, as I continued to, straight ahead.

Kate and Seabold's unpredictable journey around the stony terrace gave rise to a certain fascination. It was difficult to tell who was leading whom, unless it was Dalrymple's spirited attempt to avoid the instrument's balky keys that was manipulating them both.

"Where did he go, your Cousin Col?"

"No one knows."

"Is it possible your sister has had word from him?"

Jenny frowned.

"Why should *she* have word from him especially?"

"No reason at all."

"He disappeared one day. Packed up and left. Buttercup hadn't been watered. That is how we knew. She cried so."

"Your turn, Grandfather!" Seabold called.

I attempted to remain standing, but they pulled me forward and impelled me into Kate's arms, while Seabold led out a blushing Mrs. Thomas. Dalrymple resumed his concert, shifting, I noted, to a more stately tune.

"Your Lordship must excuse me," Kate whispered as we made our careful progress over skittering pebbles and the stray daisy. "I have no idea what I am doing."

"Nonsense. The boy has taught you well."

"This is all so unexpected."

"The rejuvenescence of his interest, you mean?"

"Master Seabold and his friend appeared at our back door one day and practically carried us off."

"Yet you are not displeased."

"I do not know," she said, as much to herself as in answer to my question. "I had thought . . ."

"Thought what?"

Worry deepened her prettiness, giving it a complexity it lacked before.

"You had thought his interest a passing fancy?"

"My father likens your stay with us to the King visiting."

"Does he really?"

"Yes. The King of France, though. Do you resemble him?"

"There is no King of France. They cut off his head."

"Oh. Then why—?"

"A bit of advice, my dear: young men are idiots." I mimed to the mental defectives in question the innocent smile of one engaged in ballroom blandishments. "When they do not call, when they fail to even pen a note, you must not assume it to mean anything other than their flea-like attention has been momentarily diverted."

"I am sure Master Seabold has been very busy, what with nursing you back to health. And then Mr. Dalrymple's visit."

". . . busy being an idiot," I corrected. "I had rather hoped you would help him overcome that condition."

"I beg your pardon?"

"I had hoped you would cure him of his ignorance, school him in the basic essentials of life."

"Whatever do you mean? What could I possibly teach him?"

"What indeed? Nothing so terrible, of that I am sure. Perhaps there are areas in which you are more experienced. Areas in which he needs instruction."

So imperceptibly had our conversation moved from frivolity to seriousness that we failed to notice the music's end, Dalrymple having concluded his playing with an elaborate flourish.

"Brava," he called appreciatively, as the ladies were encouraged to bow.

Kate broke away from me. Although she managed to conceal her distress, I noticed her eyes were unable to meet my own.

Doubtless you think me cruel, being so coarse and suggestive. But why mince words when everyone's future is at stake? She is no longer a maiden and Seabold is . . . perhaps no longer a boy but more manned than man, I fear. Were she to display some of the same earthy passions that so singed my ears at Greenwillows, he might well be led away from perverse temptation back to the straight and narrow. I feel it incumbent upon myself that he at least be given the opportunity, seeing as how Dalrymple's unexpected return was all my doing.

The remainder of the afternoon passed quickly. I allowed myself to be lulled by the chatter of the young, so soothing in its inconsequence. Thomas, I could see, was eager to engage in another *tête-à-tête*, but I managed to keep clear of him. When it was time to go, I waved away their offers of transportation, pointing out how comparatively easy the journey downhill would be. I was about to set off when Seabold returned from packing the uneaten provisions.

"Grandfather?" he asked quietly, "would you come and have a look at this?"

With no branches or tree trunks to hold onto, negotiating the naked side of the Knob was not as easy. Reluctantly, I took his arm as we approached the area where the horses had been tethered.

"Is it the blanket?" I asked, unwilling to let irritation sully what had been an otherwise enjoyable day. "Because you can tell Cook, when you get home, that I employed it up until the very moment I left."

Dalrymple was squatting by Episkidon's rear right fetlock while the horse, in obvious pain, hobbled to and fro on three hooves.

"What have you done?" I demanded. "Was he all right climbing the road? Which one of you rode him?"

"I did," Seabold said calmly. "He was fine. You know how sure-footed he is. We rode slowly to keep pace with the carriages, didn't we Lucas?"

He looked to his friend for confirmation.

"Here," was all Dalrymple replied, pointing to the pastern.

We both came closer. The poor brute neighed in alarm, rearing up as high as he could. Fleur echoed his concern, tugging at her lead.

"See the blood."

On a white horse it is particularly striking when a tendon is cut. A single telltale crimson stain trickles down. If one is being surreptitious, of course, one wipes the evidence away. Such was not the case here.

"A bee sting?" Seabold hazarded. "Or . . . a wheel's sharp edge?"

"No." I could feel night descending, though it was still quite light. At these elevations the air is so thin. "He has been lamed. Deliberately. By a knife."

May 19

The sprightly music Dalrymple played haunts my ears. To range freely over past, present and future as if they were clusters of notes, to knit from such composite experience a tune. If only I, too, could do that, as doubtless I did throughout the greater part of my life without even being aware. It is, after all, the simple art of living.

But at some point the world came to resemble one of those mechanical player contraptions whose keys depress themselves while one struggles to keep up, while one mimes performing a melody not of one's own choosing that will proceed just as inexorably without one's aid. And now the roll itself has gone askew, feeds into the maw of the works at a tilt. The chords that issue are no chords at all. I can hear behind them clicks, whirrs, the grate of metal on wood and . . . how long before the sound of thick paper, tearing?

The chill I acquired the evening of the picnic has become a full-fledged fever. Cook, in revenge for my having failed to use her blanket then, has ordered the bed piled high with them now. Sweating and confused, I fancy myself the young majesty in "The Princess and the Pea," working my way down, layer after layer, to the small essential irritant that will explain all.

I, a princess?

No, that is not right.

Yet the image of a girl tormented stays stubbornly before me.

She swam in the Tym, caught cold, and died. All in the span of three weeks, my first term at Oxford. Mother saw fit not to tell me until it was too late. Her excuses varied from fearing interruption of my studies to insufficiently grasping the gravity of the situation. I was summoned home only for the funeral.

"I thought it right she join Father," she announced, on the carriage ride back from the station.

Since her mourning of the latter had never officially ended, there were no outward signs of this new tragedy. Her veil, within the shuttered confines, was raised only enough to allow the inevitable ebony holder.

"Placed next to him, you mean?"

"Space at the sepulcher being at a premium, I per-suaded Canon Tillyard to unseal the most recent tomb."

"Put *with* him?" I turned in horror. "Her still fresh flesh dumped on his crumbling bones?"

"Really William, when did you become so dramatic? Have you joined the Theatrical Society?"

The "sepulcher" was a family mausoleum built some centuries back. It housed all manner of relations and had grown, over the years, quite cramped. Even then it was considered, well, I suppose uninhabitable is not the right word, though that conveys the general sense.

"What of yourself? Where will you sleep?"

"Not in that dank slab, thank you. I have a spot picked out on the high ground between the last yew tree and the statue of Saint George."

"Where Sir Geoffrey Grafton lies?"

She blew out a jet of smoke with an amused chuckle.

"So that is the fruit of your maudlin ramblings. You have acquainted yourself with the residents of the churchyard?"

"I consider it . . . reading," I said uncertainly, for I had in no conscious sense committed to memory all the local dead.

Yet at that moment they appeared before me, ordered in their wavering rows of stone so we, the poor living, could try and impose some sense on their senseless passing.

"Sir Geoffrey's people, if any still exist, are long scattered. None are listed in the parish registry. Canon Tillyard has been most appreciative, by contrast, of our support. He has eight children, you know. Nine, if you count that cross-eyed boy who resembles the Bishop."

"So he has agreed to move a monument?"

"When viewed from above, the distance will not seem so great. I am sure Sir Geoffrey will have no trouble retrieving his earthly form when Gabriel blows his trumpet."

"And Angela, what will she see at the Second Coming, when her eyes open?"

"What she saw in life, I fear," Mother murmured sadly. "I am surprised you object. Surely it is what she would have wanted, to spend all eternity by his side."

We rode some distance in silence. I was not even aware of her tears until she wiped them angrily away.

"Why?" I asked helplessly.

"A woman's heart is susceptible to first impression. Like wax. For some, all subsequent passions simply inhabit the mold made by their predecessor. For others, your sister among them, I fear, the organ of affection fixes into an artifact that can receive no further stress."

"Whereas your heart was of a more resilient nature."

"Be thankful I had one," she retorted, "to sacrifice for my son's well-being."

Did you sin not just as an individual but as a race? As a nation?

Did you think yourself above God? Did you think you could dispense with Him entirely and let your actions be ruled by "reason" alone? What arrogance! Or was it the opposite? Did you all too credulously believe the sanctimonious men of the pulpit, yield to their calls for blind faith and conformity? Did you allow yourself to be used by the greedy and powerful? Which was it? A bit of both, I'll wager. Our ages are not so different, queer mixes of sophistication and naiveté. You wake to find your name synonymous with bloodshed and misery, with the suffering of others, the world regarding you as perpetrator of evils you must one day answer for. You.

So you have fled to what you mistakenly suppose a simpler time, "hiding out," as it were, from your grim present. But you cannot escape. Your sins will find you, indeed they have sent you here, whether to learn a lesson or simply suffer a more exquisite form of torture I cannot say. I am hardly all-knowing, just another poor befuddled fool such as yourself. But I have lived long enough to understand there is no succor to be found below, that payment for such debts is exacted not in a never-never land of cloud-platforms and fiery pits, but at the breakfast table, in the bed's rumpled sheets, under the pitiless glare of the afternoon sun.

Fever has burned away the last impediment. I now see bits of future as clairvoyantly clear as the recoveries I have made of the past. They are just as suspect, I suppose, in their particulars, but the essence behind them is not. You have sinned—wittingly or no—against the light. There is no escape because it is *who you are*. That is the terrible truth about sin, at bottom it is nothing more than self-recognition. So the front page of the *Times* (or whatever modern-day equivalent you subscribe to), no matter how carefully ironed by your mechanical manservant, resembles an undulating mirror on some seaside pier, showing a bloated, leering, unsettlingly recognizable monster: yourself as reflected in the events your age has spawned, a portrait of your diseaséd soul, well-intentioned perhaps, but blundering and ignorant, stained with blood, ripe for judgment.

There is no need to thank me. These fits of clarity come and all I can do is set them down. It is as much an act of exorcism as warning.

What's that you say? My seeing the future is impossible?

I can only argue that, to me, it appears equally impossible my seeing the past as I do, both existing only in the moment of their apprehension. Encroaching mortality has loosened my hold on the everyday.

You dismiss my words with an uneasy laugh. That is your right. Ignore these visions at your peril, though, for they are real, as real as anything.

Men took Episkidon to the knacker's yard. Was it yesterday? No. Several days back. I heard angry neighing under my window as they tried to walk him up the plank.

Do not let it happen here, I prayed, shivering beneath the mountain of damp coverlets.

In the end, the wheels rattled off and took with them the truest friend I ever had.

How do they do it? With a blade across the throat, I recall being told. In a specially constructed narrow stall to prevent him from bolting. With a bucket held underneath. Why? Why a bucket? To catch the blood.

I must stop rambling this way, clutching the page with palsied hands, wiping sweat from my clammy brow. I must try and make sense of things.

Col. Col Woodforde. He thought it Seabold's mount, never having seen myself on the horse. Thus his hatred was misdirected. Or was it? Fleur, I imagine, grieves opposite the empty stall. Otherwise, life here has resumed. To the women we said nothing, inventing an unfortunate stumble on a loose bit of scree. Or blaming age perhaps. I hardly remember, so confused is my mind regarding the last part of the expedition. Indeed, how I got home, my subsequent chill, the hours leading up to this one, are a jumble of impressions not glued together with the unthinking mortar we use in our everyday recounting. For instance, I am haunted by the sense that I met him again, here in the Hall, though at what hour of day or night I cannot say. I caught a glimpse of him closing a door that led to the servants' corridor and pursued him through that mirror-world that provides solidity to our own. Unlike the downstairs, with its ordered rooms and cleared surfaces, the network of carpetless hallways has never appealed to me. It has a deliberately ugly nature, with wires tacked to the wall, each leading to a coil-sprung bell, and is lined with an elephants' graveyard of broken-down furniture.

"What are you doing here?" I called, when once again he showed no inclination to stop. "This is not her home."

At these words he paused, still with his back to me, and twisted slightly to peer over his shoulder.

"Kate," I went on, realizing what had snared his attention. "She is the one you are looking for, is she not?"

It was a murky corner forming an alcove before more stairs. Even so, the grin his white teeth made seemed to glow, as if supplied by an unknown source of illumination.

"You think because you left your mark on her that she belongs to you? But you took advantage," I remonstrated. "She was given no opportunity to refuse. She was a mere child."

I was perhaps ten paces away. I sensed I could not draw closer without making him flee.

"A child," he sneered. "You think she had no say in the matter? You think it was all on me?"

"Leave us in peace. Your master has offered you adequate compensation. Take it and go."

The teeth flashed. When he answered, he spoke of quite another.

"What do you know of my Master?"

"Quit these parts." I was surprised to hear a note of pleading in my voice. "Save your own soul. Do not give in to the forces that threaten your salvation."

He looked about wildly as if I had summoned a demon, then spat and deliberately smeared the gob into the dusty floorboards with his boot.

"A what?" Rosewater asked this morning, when I whispered my request.

"Poison," I repeated. "The deadliest imaginable. Fast-acting, with no taste or odor."

"Your Lordship has been reading too many serialized fictions. Lie still, please. My brief is to heal. What makes you think I would have knowledge of such insidious compounds?"

"Come, come. We all know how your people used to lure Gentile children to their deaths in order to obtain enough blood necessary for preparation of the Sacramental Matzo. Let go of me, sir."

"So you wish to redress some mythical slaughter of the innocents at this late date?"

"Don't be daft. It is for the villain who lamed my horse!"

He continued to try and restrain my attempt to rise.

"And on account of my ancestors' rumored crimes you assume I am willing to assist in the commission of a modern-day murder?"

"One does not murder a rabid dog. One puts him down. One *acts*, finally, after a lifetime of hesitation."

"This is a hopeful sign, my Lord, your attempting to push my arm back in so forceful a fashion, but too much agitation may result in—"

Where the strength came from I cannot say. All I know is I found myself sole possessor of the field, or what passed for a field, the stale air and clutter of the sickroom, while Rosewater observed me from a safe distance, ruefully rubbing his shoulder.

"My horse," I repeated. "He killed my horse."

"Your grandson told me the beast stumbled. That he was quite aged."

"Yes, well of course he would say that. Lies we manufacture for others quickly become the accepted currency of our own minds. But I see the truth."

"I must caution your Lordship against doing anything rash."

"When you reach my age it is impossible to be rash. The most spontaneous-seeming step has the consideration of nearly nine decades behind it."

"Seeking out a phantom who may or may not have committed a crime, with the intention of 'putting him down . . .'"

"Did I say that?" I laughed. "You have a most peculiar talent for listening."

"It is part of my profession. I sometimes think it the principal asset a physician may possess."

"I am not sure the offhand remarks of others are all that revealing."

"Nevertheless, if I thought your statements contained any substance I would be obliged to report them to Mr. Justice Beaumont."

"There is hardly need for that. What you witnessed was only a fit of pique. Rest assured I am not going off to commit general mayhem."

He regarded me with a cold, calculating expression.

"You have had a setback."

"Nonsense. It was merely a fever. Now that it has broken, I feel my old self again."

"The limp is more pronounced, as if it were you, rather than your horse, who had suffered injury. Perhaps that is why you harp so on the imagined attack."

"What a poetic notion for a man of science."

"I only mean to suggest that your brain is confused, that it is struggling to make sense of what is happening to it and in so doing may have lost touch with—"

"Please keep your godless fingers out of my brain. Next they will be squeezing and poking at my immortal soul and *that* is an area where, despite your family's three generations of mouthing alien doctrine, I know for a fact you are still forbidden trespass."

I regretted this outburst at soon as it was made but could hardly go back on it, standing there, panting and trembling in the center of the room.

He seemed to come to some decision and proceeded to close his bag.

"Are there no medications you intend to leave?"

"None, my Lord."

"No little pills or nauseating draughts?" I pressed.

"I would counsel moderation," he finally pronounced, "in both diet and deed."

This evening, we had an early thunderstorm. I managed to make my way up to the rooftop and huddled there under a small canopy-like structure I barely remembered existing. Clouds approached, darkening the sky to pewter. Treetops, still young enough to contain two distinct shades of green, were blown inside-out, baring tender undersides, losing their shape.

The door opened and Mrs. Ellis emerged . . . to deliver a grand scolding and chase me downstairs, I thought at first; but it was clear from her surprise that she too had come on her own, drawn by the same anticipation as myself.

"Sweeping down from the north." She shivered as I made room for her to sit beside me. "Would your Lordship like the end of my shawl?"

"Thank you, no," I answered. "As you see, I came prepared."

"I'll wager you gave the moths quite a fright when you resurrected that old thing."

It was the only judgment she passed on my muffler, and made in a pleasant enough tone.

We watched Mann fight the wind rushing to secure a shutter that had come loose. A bird, late getting home, hurtled sideways past our vision. It was unusual to see an animal so robbed of its natural grace.

"The gentlemen?" I asked.

"In the parlour playing that game."

"Backgammon."

"Yes."

"Not with the ladies, then?"

"Not tonight. I imagine Squire Thomas is in a panic over his wheat."

"You think there will be hail?"

"The air is wet enough. And with this cold . . ."

I drew the threadbare tweed of my jacket closer. A distant rumble announced what was to come.

"Has the boy shown any inclination to speak to you, Mrs. Ellis?"

"Speak to me about what?"

"His plans. The future. His intentions."

"Those are hardly fit subjects for Master Seabold to be discussing with a servant, my Lord. In such matters I expect he would come to you."

"We are all servants to the young."

"True enough," she nodded, "though they hardly seem to know it."

"I wondered if he had been given news. News that he could not share with me and so might have unburdened himself to you, instead."

"Nothing of that nature, no," she said briskly.

Her hands, folded in her lap, still bore their wedding band. I was reminded of bark, how over the years it comes to a kind of accommodation with whatever foreign object has been affixed to it, until rusty metal and scarred wood grow inseparable.

"The doctor," she allowed, "did come down for a cup of tea before he left."

"Did he now?"

"Said he was parched."

"And what did he talk about?"

"Listened mostly. He did ask about your mother, what I had heard. Her end particularly. Your father's as well . . . but mostly 'the maternal side,' he called it."

"My mother and father's manner of death? A family history, then."

"I suppose."

"So it was you he spoke to."

"Not in so many words. I told you, mostly he sat."

We stared into the encroaching blackness. Bits of stick and leaf struck the roof, advance guard of a much greater army. Coming from the arctic regions, the air had a cleansing chill.

"I suppose it difficult," I tried again, "for a medical man to divine how much knowledge of his condition a patient wishes to receive."

"Only God knows our fate," she said sententiously, "and only by prayer can we know God. So the only true knowledge of our condition is to be found in worship."

"Why Mrs. Ellis, I had no idea you were so devout."

"Your mother," she turned to me with an unusually direct gaze, "they say her end was particularly terrible. Is that true?"

I was surprised. It was the wind perhaps, disarranging her hair, which I noted for the first time was not protected by her cap, or perhaps it was the lazy cast of habit blown from my own tired eyes. I was surprised at how old she appeared.

"Terrible? It was terrible for her because of the active life she had led up until that point. But in all the deaths I have witnessed there has never been a *happy* one. Why do you ask?"

Just then lightning—always a surprise, no matter how much one expects it, always making one jump—split the sky, followed by an enormous clap of thunder.

"Come," I said, helping her up.

Her prevoyance had been correct. Small icy balls were bouncing with savage buoyancy all around us. From below I heard the tinkle of broken glass. Sheltering her as best I could, we made our way to the door. Once there, though, she paused and clutched my muffler, enunciating clearly, trying to make herself heard over the racket of wind and hail.

"I fear for your Lordship's health."

"Why? What did the doctor tell you?"

"Nothing. But the questions he asked . . ."

"Perhaps they were posed in the spirit of curiosity."

"What will become of us, my Lord?"

"The boy will rise to the occasion. I did, and I was no better prepared than he."

A terrific sheet of white illuminated our forms in stark detail. She appeared to be crying.

"Surely there is something we can do!"

"We must go back inside," I shouted, bundling her out of the maelstrom.

Before turning and taking myself away, though, I gave one last look at the destruction. There was something grimly satisfying in finding nature's ordered universe subject to the same chaos as our own supposedly rational minds.

Let it all come down, I thought.

In a gesture reminiscent of childhood, I stuck out my tongue and caught on its very tip a ball of hail, hard as shot.

Time then wandered, lost its purpose and flooded the fields. Tufts of grass dotted its surface. Tree trunks rose straight out of their own quivering reflections. Such was the period after Angela's passing. The years stretched on, interminable and formless. Though outwardly I continued to grow, my true progress was of a more spreading, soaking nature. Into this stagnant pool, Albemarle's wire fell with a splash. I read it once before placing it casually on the fire, having inherited more of Mother's blasé duplicitousness than I cared to admit.

"What is it?" she demanded.

"One of my school chums, asking to visit."

"What shall you answer?"

"I shall tell him no."

The need to pen a reply provided an excuse for cutting short our excruciating hour together.

"Why not, Billy?" she called after me. "It would do you good to have friends."

I kept my back ramrod straight, maintaining a carefully measured tread, as if her eyes were on me still, though that, of course, was impossible. It was ironic how her being confined to one room suggested her spirit, by contrast, roamed free, observing me from distant vantage points and cobwebbed corners. I performed veritable melodramas of deception to an absent audience, shielded what I wrote from unseeing eyes.

Come at once, I scrawled on the form, aware that at least the pounding of my heart need not be concealed. *I need you here. All is forgiven.*

"Billy?" Her voice traveled down the stairs she herself could not.

I shut my ears to it, and went in search of the telegraph boy.

"Billy? Are you there?"

Creeping Paralysis proved a most aptly-named malady. She was reduced to just such a teetering, shuffling, painfully slow form of locomotion, before imprisonment in wheelchair, *chaise longue,* and then bed; for "creeping" described its progress within her body as well, inexorable yet invisible, a glacier engulfing an Alpine village.

As she was thus entombed alive, an awkward tenderness began to manifest itself. It confused, I saw, the servants, accustomed to her imperious commands, how she now framed every order as a question. ("Might I . . . have the drapes drawn?") It confused myself as well, the sudden concern she showed for my well-being.

"Her name is Maud. The Duchess says she is awfully sweet. Would you like to see a photograph?"

I noted, more than the artificially posed girl, her eyes uplifted in a "soulful" gaze, the signature of the portraitist discretely penned against the black of the background in white ink.

"A fetching girl," she supplied, when it was clear I would have no comment. "And . . . awfully sweet."

"He cannot sleep here," I muttered, betraying my thoughts.

"Who cannot? Your friend? Have you changed your mind? Of course he can sleep here. There are your old

137

quarters, for starters. Just ask that they be aired. Or if you wish to impress him with something more grand—"

"Did you hear?" I asked, and sprang up before she could answer, striding off in search of an imagined messenger.

We exchanged a flurry of telegrams. How well I remember the emphasis I laid on each word sent and received. The crumpled forms. The parsed phrases. "Albemarle" versus just "A." The cryptic significance with which I invested each no doubt arbitrary method of signature.

It was finally agreed we meet in the village, where he could alight from the 12:06 and re-embark on the 4:18. (How like Biblical verses are the times of long since discontinued trains.) It was mutual, I recall, our wishing to keep his visit private. Perhaps he had heard of Mother's affliction, or perhaps there was a residual twinge of guilt over his behavior towards Angela. All such speculation was supplied by myself, of course. His replies to my florid and expensive inquiries were increasingly terse.

What did I expect from him? Something so giant as to be beyond my conception. To me, he had always existed outside the laws of our closed-off world, swooping down to offer fantastic opportunities the very nature of which I remained unaware. Unaware yet in dire need of.

I expected, in short, to be rescued.

"Does it have a name?" Dalrymple asked this morning.

"Eh?" I murmured, still recovering from a poor night during which I was tormented by memories that were not quite dreams but not real, either.

"The boat. We intend to launch it soon, mark its maiden voyage, or whatever a second maiden voyage is called after a three-quarter-century hiatus. Most of the paint has peeled away and we are giving it a fresh coat. In your day, what was its name?"

"In my day, it had none. There was no need."

"A simpler time," Seabold offered.

"Hardly."

"Then we must have a christening," Dalrymple resolved, "and uncork a bottle of champagne."

Seabold absented himself to deal with estate matters, something he has been doing more and more of lately, leaving me to watch his friend bone a finnan haddie.

"Of the three, you are the most," I realized.

"Undoubtedly," he answered; and then, after taking another bite, continued: "The most what?"

"In love."

"Ah."

"And so the most careful about not revealing it. Because of what he means to you."

"You presume to know my innermost feelings. Yet when we first met," he pointed out, "you confused me with someone else."

"I confused you with him, perhaps because I sensed on your part such a complete longing to identify with the object of your infatuation."

"Spoken like a man who has done his own fair share of feeling."

"Have I?" I wondered. "If so, I am left with little to show for it."

"Nonsense. You inspire devotion, albeit of an odd sort."

"But not from you."

"Good God, no. That is why you enjoy speaking to me so much."

Mann entered and left.

"She is a good girl," he resumed, upon the servant's departure, as if we had continued to converse uninterruptedly all the while and were now further along, "above her station in manners, grace, and, if I may run the risk of sounding snobbish, in decency as well."

"Decency! I am surprised to hear you say that. You recall I told you the very opposite, your first night here."

"Yes, but since then I have spent many more nights at Upton and befriended many more of its residents—your charming girl Mary, for instance—enough to see that, in these soft southern counties, what passes for decency is more honored in the breeches than the observance, if you take my meaning."

"Are you going to leave, then? Renounce your interests? Withdraw from the field and allow the boy to conduct a normal life?"

"Could I," he mused, "even if I wanted to, being, as you suggest, so in thrall? Besides, what of *her* heart? Is it not pledged to another?"

"The one I saw her with, you mean?"

"Yes."

"Not likely. He did her great harm."

"Love does greatly harm," he shrugged. "You said as much yourself just now, when limning my own predicament."

"No. This one is more demon than man. He is a lewd lascivious hairy brute."

"Hmm. I certainly see the appeal."

"Kate!" I exclaimed, gripped suddenly by my own description of the continued danger she is in, every moment I do not act.

"What about her?" Seabold asked, returning with a sheaf of papers.

"Are you planning one of your excursions with the ladies this afternoon?"

"Not today, no."

"I need to speak to her."

"Can you travel?"

"Of course I can travel," I answered peevishly. "How do you think I got down here? Via magic carpet?"

"I meant in the carriage, as far as Saint Bartholomew's."

"Why on earth would she be at Saint Bartholomew's?"

They looked at me, pityingly.

"Oh, it is Sunday, then?"

. . . for I see now, looking back over these most recent entries, that I have ceased to note when they were written, that I have lost track completely of the days.

Thus it was that, for the first time in over a year, I attended Service, bringing tears to the eyes of Mrs. Ellis, who, along with the rest of the staff, occupied one of the rear pews. Our private bench was dusty through long neglect. I was surprised at how little my attitude toward the ceremony itself had changed. Despite whatever newfound urgency the current lad's warnings of hell-fire and damnation ought to have taken on, I never felt more sure I was witnessing an infantile puppet show, that any house of worship was a place where one sheltered *from* God, rather than sought Him out. Even the stained glass struck me as filtering His blinding essence from Our cowardly eyes.

After reviewing the preposterous rigmarole of the prickly-tempered Hebrew and his wish to suffer muti-lation, the baby-faced chap issued a few more random admonishments and exited stage right, as it were, only to pop magically back up again outside the doors, greeting us as we emerged blinking in the sunshine.

"Your LORDSHIP," he shouted, extending his hand while simultaneously attempting something between a curtsey and a bow.

Damage from the recent winds was evident in the sad form of a nest blown to the ground. I stooped to pick it up.

"It has been a long ABSENCE," he bawled, enunci-ating certain words with unnatural clarity, assuming I was a deaf idiot. "Of course I was well aware of your Lord-ship's INFIRMITIES and had even considered journeying out one day to Upton with the thought you might require SPIRITUAL GUIDANCE."

Three eggs were wedged at the bottom. Intact, I con-firmed, stroking gently their miraculous light-blue shells.

"Robin Red Breast."

"I beg your Lordship's PARDON?"

"Yes, tolerable-good sermon," I said, remembering my manners. "Unfortunate fellow, Christ. Bit of a whiner at the end, what?"

"My wife and I would be honored if you would grace our table at TEA, this afternoon."

But I had already spotted Kate, gathered with some of the other young misses at a spot upwind from the assembled conveyances. A pretty picture they formed, though she stood out as a swan among geese.

It is not just her looks, I remember thinking at the time, but her utterly unguarded expression, an openness of both spirit and mien.

"Good morning, your Lordship," she said, while the other girls scattered in terror. "Oh, how pretty."

I followed her gaze and saw I was still holding the nest.

"This? Doomed. A night's repast for some cat or fox."

"Father says you caught a chill returning that day after our lovely picnic. I am so sorry."

"Where is he, child?"

"Father? Over by the—"

"Where is Col Woodforde?"

She did not react at first, save that her smile froze, then slowly faded.

"I saw you with him in the stables, that night at Green-willows. I know what it is you do, what he makes you do. And I know he is here still, tormenting his victims: you, Episkidon, myself. None of us is safe until I deal with him."

"Col?" she faltered. "He is gone. He left more than two weeks ago. No one knows where."

"I have seen him since. I have spoken with him. Are you telling me you have not?"

"No, my Lord." She shook her head. "As for what you saw that night . . ."

"Speak no more of it."

Evading her glistening eyes, I looked down and found in wonderment that I *still* held the bird's nest, despite my attempts to let go, to shake it free.

"You must think me beneath contempt."

"On the contrary, I know you to be a good girl."

"No! I am not!"

"He forced himself upon you. You are the weaker sex and have no say in such matters. That is why I must find him and—"

"—said he loved me," she whispered.

Her shoulders heaved.

I was conscious of the entire village, while feigning not to, watching us from a discreet distance.

"He spoke so sweetly. At first. It was only later, when there was no going back, that I discovered his true nature."

"Is there no secret place he marked out as his own?" I went on, attempting to ignore what I had heard. "A hidden cave? Some impenetrable thicket?"

"He is gone," she repeated stubbornly.

"But I told you, I saw him."

"Your Lordship is imagining things. I am sorry to say it, but your Lordship does so more and more. Everyone says."

"Everyone says what?"

"That your Lordship sees what is not!"

A small price to pay for seeing what *is*. That is what I should have answered. Instead of standing there, gazing vacantly, as she hurried off.

The weather mocks me by approaching perfection. Today, the terrace's mundane view is that of a Promised Land to which I am denied entry.

There is a blanket on my legs.

I fell this morning, an event of no great importance to myself but apparently engendering a ripple of concern throughout the Hall. Only my most strenuous objections prevented Rosewater from once again being summoned. Instead I was forced to accept a dose of Mrs. Ellis' Wallflower Infusion, a glass of hot swamp which, when viewed at eye level, hosts strange translucent creatures scuttling crabwise through its depths.

Though just now, when I mildly observed as much, she indignantly denied the very possibility of their existence.

Amusing, what we do not allow ourselves to see, except in moments of sickness or despair.

I *can* get up. It is more an overpowering sense of not-wanting-to.

I do not wish this Journal to become a mere catalogue of symptoms, and so from hereon will scrupulously refrain from noting the various aches and pains which dictate my physical existence. Or rather free me from it, as my mind ranges far and wide, a falcon at last untethered.

Strange, who turns out to be good with the sick. Seabold I would have thought ill-equipped to deal with the more unsavory aspects of care, yet he proves surprisingly adept at playing nursemaid, suppressing any winces of disgust he may feel, handling me in an easy yet not over-familiar fashion. Mrs. Ellis, on the other hand, despite her vaunted skills at managing, appears strangely nervous, rushing through her tasks as if to make a quick escape, answering my questions distractedly and asking none of her own in return.

Good manners will be my downfall.

Today I had a note from Thomas requesting an immediate interview. Since I could not very well go myself, I reluctantly agreed to receive him here. He came along with Jenny, but first struck up a conversation with Mann, of all people, about certain repairs that need be made to the Hall's drainpipes, during which time the girl spoke to me in a low voice about the true reason for their visit.

"She will not get out of bed. She will not eat. That is why he has come. He thinks her lovesick."

"Is she not?"

"It is because of what you told her outside the church last Sunday."

"I told her nothing."

"She says you *saw* her."

"That was a private conversation between myself and your sister."

"Is it true then, that you saw her with Col?"

"I saw her being attacked," I corrected, keeping a careful eye on Thomas, who was acting as if he was already, through the marriage of his daughter, part-owner of the place.

"Clarence? Is he to do it? I must have a word with him first. A good man, Clarence, but . . ."

"It was not her fault," I insisted.

"It was Col's fault?"

"I cannot believe she spoke to you of such things."

"If it was Col's fault, then why did you not stop him?"

"This is not a fit subject to be discussing with a girl of your tender years. The only reason I pressed her so was because I thought she would know where Woodforde was hiding."

"He is not hiding. He is gone."

"So everyone says, but I have seen him."

"Have you?"

I smiled. Of them all, it is only she who does not treat me like a child or, worse, a piece of Dresden china that will crumble at the slightest touch.

"I have, indeed, as plain as day. Several times. He even appeared here at the Hall, harassing me during my recent illness."

"Here? But how did he get in?"

"I do not know. He seems to have the ability to pass through walls."

"Then he haunts you," she said with certainty.

"No. It is his flesh and blood I see, not his spirit."

"Flesh and blood haunt the most, do they not?"

Her solemn eyes regarded me without blinking. I looked up and that was when it happened. For one precious moment I was gazing into another's long-extinguished soul.

"Miranda?" I whispered, the syllables tasting strange on my tongue.

"What shall I tell her?"

Though it was Jenny, it was my daughter as well, and though it was Kate she had been sent by, it was Alice, too. Time and circumstance collapsed, forcing my answer to do double-duty.

". . . my . . . love," I managed to croak, though whether or not the words survived their passage into sound I cannot say.

Ever so much later.

Or is it?

"When are you leaving?"

Seabold, caught crossing the Lawn rather than taking the path, paused. I noted he had his sketchbook with him again.

"I am leaving now," he answered, "for the boathouse. We are almost ready to move down to the river. Would you like me to sit with you, Grandfather?"

"When are you leaving *here*?" I attempted to indicate Upton, the district or, possibly, if he chose to take it so, this entire segment of his life.

He turned and regarded me. I fancied I saw the faintest hint of a beard, though perhaps it was a shadow cast on his jaw.

"I have no immediate plans to leave the Hall, if that is what you mean. Why? Would you like me to? Are you sending me away?"

"I did not summon you, yet you came; therefore I see no point in attempting to send you away."

"I came because you were ill."

"Not because you had squandered your fortune? Or because you had fallen into a slough of nancy-boy perversion?"

"No," he answered steadily, "neither of those. It was, as I said, out of concern for your health."

"A health you had no way of knowing was in danger," I riposted triumphantly. "How could you, when we had barely communicated over the course of the previous year?"

"Cook saw fit to keep me informed. It was she who agreed I should come, after I put the question to her in a letter."

"So you have been conspiring behind my back."

"Yes, well you don't seem too good at accepting help when it is offered directly."

"Thomas," I sighed, realizing that I had gone totally off the rails with my initial line of inquiry, reluctant as I was to bring us round to the true subject, "has asked me to speak to you."

"Is Kate feeling better? I know she has been indisposed the past few days."

"Indisposed? She is pining, dear boy. Wondering what, if any, your intentions may be."

"And that is what Thomas wished to ascertain? My intentions?"

"He is willing to offer a great deal of money. He has 'come up,' you might say, in our negotiations. Not for the social advancement such a union represents, but because he genuinely loves his daughter and now fears for her happiness."

"Yet, as you never tire of reminding me, her father's father once carted wood."

"At this point I am more concerned for your children's children, neither of whom will exist if you continue in this bizarre attachment to another."

He made as if to go off again.

"Wait, Seabold!"

"Yes, Grandfather?"

"It is hard for me to be sincere. I sometimes fall back on a vein of gentle raillery."

"So I have noticed."

"I don't really give a hang whom you end up with, so long as the person makes you happy."

"Then why—?"

"This feeling youth has that time exists in inexhaustible supply, that no decisions need be made, no plans formulated or future considerations taken into account . . . well, it is wonderful so far as it goes but it *does* go and . . . one lands with a bit of a thump," I ended lamely. "Which is what I would like to see you cushioned against, cushioned monetarily, among other ways, before I . . ."

He came forward and sat on the grass directly before my chair. The difference in our relative heights made him seem a child again.

"What are you sketching?"

Facing it outwards, he opened the book.

There were charcoal renderings of the Tym, its rippled surface, its eddies and swells, even one of toes, seen from above, squeezing at pebbles through the swiftly moving current.

"Will you be going out on the water, then?"

"Once we launch her. Lucas still has work to do."

"Despite your fear?"

"Because of it, you would say."

"And you will invite Kate and Jenny?"

"Of course."

"Good."

"This whole business of choosing . . ."

"It is a myth," I agreed. "As soon as one is taxed with making a decision, the element of freedom dies. One realizes all one's so-called 'choices' are hydra's heads belonging to the same monstrous creature."

"What, then, would you have me do?"

"Choose a path not yet in evidence. Create one where there appears to be none."

"Is that what you did?"

"It is most emphatically what I did not do. To my discredit."

He nodded, a gesture of understanding more than assent, a promise to consider what I had said, all while continuing to display the pages, as if these tangible reminders of what he had already accomplished gave him strength, until he came at last to a different subject: his naked self, viewed in a mirror.

"Handsome lad," I allowed.

"Yes," he smiled, regaining his former manner. "Well, I shall always have *that*."

Today I determined the cause of Mrs. Ellis' reserve.

Watching as she speedily set down my luncheon (Mann having been called away), I attempted to postpone her departure by praising the effect of her most recent potion, one that enables me to pass much of the night in relative peace.

"What ingredient is it that so soothes?" I wondered. "Do I detect a hint of chamomile?"

"That," she grudgingly admitted, "and other flowers."

"Where do you find them? I hardly picture you traipsing through the woods with a basket over your arm pausing now and then to pluck some magic bloom."

"They are quite common if you know where to look."

"And how does one come by such wisdom?"

"A woman taught me when I was caring for my sainted Joseph. She lived in a cottage on the edge of Epping Forest."

"Some latter-day witch, eh?"

"A witch? No. She was a good Christian soul. The kindness she did me was beyond all measure."

"Then it was she who allowed you to ease your husband's pain when the doctors could not?"

"What does your Lordship mean by that?"

"Nothing. I merely said—"

"Of what do you accuse me?"

"Accuse you?"

"Jesus forgive me!" she sobbed.

I hardly knew what I had been getting at. Indeed, my only conscious aim had been to prolong our time together and perhaps encourage her to speak more freely, as she used to before my illness became more pronounced. Imagine my surprise, then, when all at once she fell weeping into my arms.

"Ease his pain, I did! For death is one thing but dying quite another."

"What are you talking about, woman?"

"He was in agony!" she wailed. "Begged me, he did. Begged me to help him pass over. The doctor said there was nothing more to do, that we must let the disease run its course. But Old Sally Brown, she in her tumbledown room beyond the last fields, she knew what I had come for, knew it before I even got out the words to ask."

"Then she was a better reader of minds than I, for what you say makes no apparent sense at all."

"Nightshade. What they call the Devil's Cherries. She showed me how to find it, how to extract its essence so he would slip from wakefulness to sleep, and from sleep to rest."

"Do you mean to say that you fed your husband poison?"

"I didn't feed it to him. I told him what it was, what it would do. He nodded his head (he could barely speak by then) and bade me leave. When I returned, the glass was empty and his soul . . . his soul was already ascending heavenward."

She broke into a fresh fit of lamentation.

"Why are you telling me this?"

"Because time has come round again. Don't you see? I knew it the moment the doctor asked after your mother. My blood ran cold, seeing what would be asked of me."

"Asked by whom? I have asked nothing of you."

"Not yet, but you will."

"What makes you think that?"

"Surely your Lordship does not wish to experience what her Ladyship did."

"It was a difficult time, but—"

"More than difficult, I have heard tell."

"There was," I found myself remembering, "a month at the end during which she could barely move, much less make her wishes known. I fed her with a spoon. I still recall the sound of her throat attempting to swallow, a ghastly rattle in the otherwise gruesome silence."

"It is why I was sent here," she went on gravely, regaining her composure. "So that I could one day provide you with the cure she was denied, the same as I did for Joseph."

"A cure you call it?"

"For those who suffer, yes. The cure to all that is yet to come, though for myself it will be a burden I never thought I would have to take up again. Oh the nightmares that followed!"

She has gone now, after further talk and commiseration, with much swearing on both our parts to tell no one what passed between us. I hesitate, even, to write down as much as I have, though my by-now wild scrawl makes the likelihood of a stranger extracting any sense from the above quite remote.

We met at the entrance, whether by design or chance I cannot now remember. It was a sunken door. Mounds of earth on either side of the columns and pediment loomed, their turfy hair level with our own.

"Have you a key?" he asked.

I did. Now how is that possible, unless we had planned it? Perhaps in those days I carried one with me, a morbid keepsake. That would certainly have fit my mood at the time. The heavy swollen oak, with its superfluous iron bars, scraped over stone as we pushed it back.

"Rot," he sniffed.

"Because it is so recent," I explained. "The last deposition."

"Not all that recent."

"A body takes its time."

"You come here often, then?"

Cramped, I believe I called it. But there remained a central aisle so that new stone boxes could be assembled, when needed, on the already-laid plinths; and there was also an ornamental chapel, or at least a "sacred spot" where one could ostensibly lose one's self in contemplation. A tablet there held some sort of inscription, oddly faded. The marble it was written on had gone soft and cushiony so the text more resembled minute creases in a pillow. Really, the crypt was more claustrophobic than cramped. One kept one's arms close to one's sides so as not to inadvertently touch or brush against anything.

Though Albemarle, I recall, acted in the opposite manner. He ran his fingers along every dirty, mouldering surface, stooped to blow away dust and trace the dates of my long-departed ancestors.

"I take an interest in genealogy. You are quite ancient," he announced.

"My line, you mean."

"Yes. You."

I was still taking advantage of every opportunity afforded to cast a surreptitious glance, cataloguing the changes that had taken place. He had coarsened to a shocking degree. Not in ways I could convince myself to find endearing, such as a *gravitas*-enhancing girth or a more stately posture, though those were in evidence as well. No, it was more as if a parodist's pencil had passed over his features and brought out the heretofore hidden flaws lurking in each. The bridge of his nose had "bubbled up," while his mouth, by contrast, had grown thin and mean. His hair, once plentiful, had yielded to an oddly artificial crop of curls, all the same length, in rows, which ended abruptly in a sweating circle of pink. But it was his eyes, where I most desperately sought recognition, that had undergone the most violent change, paradoxically by remaining the same as the rest of him had grown, and so been reduced to piggish pinpoints directing tiny beams of inquiry on whatever they were trained.

"And this would be," he puffed, still squatting, waddling from one tomb to the next, "the sixth Earl."

"Father, yes."

"I had a great respect for your father."

The seam running up the back of his trousers was about to split. I looked away and kicked at an unfortunate leaf that had been blown in along with us and would now be doomed to suffer here for all eternity.

"He gave sage advice," Albemarle went on, straightening slowly, holding the small of his back.

"Father gave you advice? When?"

"I often visited him upstairs in his study."

"His cell."

"We would discuss all sorts of things. He was a fount of wisdom."

"He was never such a fount for me, more a cataract of abuse I was forced to pass under if I wished to get anywhere."

"I sensed he had a great store of paternal wisdom he longed to impart. My father, too, I found a taciturn fellow. Perhaps in our class it is difficult to be kind to one's own, knowing he will one day assume all that is yours."

"What sort of things did Father tell you?"

"Commonplaces, I suppose. It was more the act of passing-on that made them memorable." He nodded to the tomb. "She is in here as well?"

"So you heard."

"I remember there being talk at the time."

"Yes, Angela is there."

"Why is there no record?"

"Mother says the stone would have to be replaced rather than recut. I imagine she is loath to spend the funds."

"So your estate is still undercapitalized. That was one of the factors my parents objected to."

"Why you didn't marry her, you mean?"

He turned to me with a look of kindness. It was the cruelest blow yet, the benign, comradely attitude he assumed.

"I had the deepest feelings for your sister, William. I would have ignored my parents' qualms, had I been given the opportunity."

"But you didn't, did you?" I replied sullenly. "You stole off like a thief, to go 'grouse-hunting in Scotland, as far as Galashiels, if that is where the winged tribe takes me.'"

The hurt. It was amazing how the hurt, so carefully preserved, could be unwrapped and prove as fresh as the moment it was initially inflicted. I saw even he was surprised at how precisely I quoted long forgotten words, some pleasantry dashed off on now-yellowed notepaper.

"In fact, I went off to nurse my wounded pride, although the birds did bear the brunt of my suffering, I admit."

"The brunt of your suffering? And what of ours? Do you know how many years afterwards I fell asleep to the sound of muffled sobs? Do you know how, even today, I sometimes wake to their distant echo?"

"She was troubled."

"She was *wounded*, mortally, by a cad who toyed with her affections."

"No, William." He laid his hand on my shoulder. "It was she who turned me down. I see by your reaction that you were never told."

My "reaction," as he called it, was not to anything he said, words being the barely intelligible rumble of thunder compared to the bolt of electricity that shot through me at his touch. I have been told women feel this way at moments, when simple contact leads to something more profound. Well, perhaps I am a woman underneath, or was, for that brief instant in time.

He, however—no doubt this was the chief difference between his current plodding self and the quicksilver tempter I had enshrined in my memory—remained oblivious to the effect he was creating.

"I proposed to her in the spring of that year. She asked for more time, which I obligingly gave her. Then your father's death intervened, which naturally held the matter in abeyance for several months. When I renewed my suit, after a decent interval, she told me in no uncertain terms it would not be granted."

"W-w-why?" I managed to stammer.

"Though her refusal was plain enough, she would not tell me the reasoning behind it, which was her right, of course. Are you unwell?"

I forced myself to turn away, sorting through the words that had been backing up in my head waiting to be assayed and answered.

"But of this she told you nothing?" he guessed.

"No."

"She swore me to secrecy, which was why I wrote in that cavalier vein, so as not to be drawn into a discussion of matters I was duty-bound to avoid. I am sorry if it caused you pain."

"Why have you come?" I asked.

"Why do you think?"

"I thought perhaps you came to pray to her for forgiveness; but from what you claim it seems you have nothing to be forgiven for. Or, I thought perhaps you came for me."

"For you?"

"Because we once . . ."

"Ah yes, we had a grand time, didn't we? As close as brothers."

It was confusing how his porcine face and vague wooly sentiments still set off in me the same thrill of a decade past, how I would have dropped anything, betrayed anyone, to obey his will in matters great and small, if only to continue inhaling that faded fragrance of time irretrievably lost, all while he felt nothing, recalled

155

nothing, was content to act as though those same memories that practically fixed the course of my own life were of events that, in his mind, had never even taken place.

"I came," he said, changing his manner, becoming more formal and hearty, "to see if I could interest you in an investment opportunity."

"Money?" Mother asked.

"Some scheme to ship sugar in returning slave vessels. I did not really follow."

"Nor should you have. There is nothing sweet in the traffic of human souls."

"Indeed."

I had felt, pulling the door shut, wrestling with the ring, a sense of finality, that I was, for better or worse, grown. Nothing more could happen to me. Or it could, rather, but it would not change the fundamental elements of which my character was now composed. That process was complete.

It made sitting with Mother, formerly a fidget-inducing chore, more tolerable.

"Has he gone back on his word?" she asked anxiously.

"Who?"

"Canon Tillyard. Because there was nothing in writing, of course. It was more a wink and a nod."

"You shall rest by the statue of Saint George."

"They are always taking things from me. They promise one thing but provide quite another, the very opposite!"

"Shh. There is no need to agitate yourself."

"You will find it so, Billy. The lies they tell hold the truths they would conceal."

"Yes, Mother."

"I wish to be out in the open air, in the sunshine, not shut up in that gritty cave!"

"I will see to it, Mother."

It will happen soon. Cook, after more whispered consultations, will be persuaded to re-enact her sin. She will do so despite much weeping and dread, little realizing that this time she *saves* both her soul and another's. They will all be down by the river to christen the boat. (I have been told its name, but forgotten.) There was talk of transporting myself—in a sedan chair, of all things—but I put a stop to that. It will all unfold perfectly. Odd, how the less direct influence I am able to exert on this world, the more I see it bending inexorably towards my purposes.

He will come, once they are gone. He has been waiting to catch me alone, for am I not the only one here who still believes? The others are so convinced of his departure that he could plant himself directly in their path and they would pass unseeing right through him.

I, too, know what it is like to grow invisible.

He will appear here on the terrace. I will be surrounded by my accoutrements: the shawl-like blanket they insist on draping over me no matter how warm the day, the bell (to summon whom?), this tattered, swollen book, and the "tonic" upon which I have grown so dependent of late, Mrs. Ellis' strange soporific brew. But the one she makes for me that day will be of a different nature, designed to provide not just relief, but escape.

The boat, meanwhile, will be commencing its new life. They will struggle to drag it over grass and root, all the able-bodied men. How long has that craft languished on dry land? It is a wonder the wood has not crumbled to dust.

Will we talk? I do not know if there is much to say. I suppose we will. The hilt of his knife will poke out above his ragged belt. I shall charm and disarm him. We shall arrive at a pact with concessions made on both sides. He will promise to leave them all be and I, in turn . . . will swear to do the same. A mutual leave-taking, sealed with a toast. We shall swallow from the same glass. In fact, now that I envision the scene, I long to converse with him, after a lifetime of avoidance.

The boat floats free on the water. There will be that magic moment when the load ceases and a smooth gliding takes its place. The young ones clamber aboard. Seabold, Kate, Lucas Dalrymple, Jenny. They grasp the oars and pull. They watch the bank of the river diminish, hear shouted words of encouragement, backing their way with each stroke into a future that will only grow visible when it is passed.

Then sleep. My prayer is that my eyes stay open long enough to see him sprawled lifeless on the ground, a dragon slain. (Thus Margaret Ellis' mortal misstep, I must remind whoever is in charge, is forgiven by her aiding in the destruction of Pure Evil.) I should like my last moment on this earth, pitiful though it may appear from without, to be that of a hero, exulting.

And yours? My last moment is your first, as you close this book and set off with lively step. Rejoice, your time among the dead is done. Whatever lesson you were supposed to learn by being assigned this act of witness is finished. Now to face again the bewildering world, with its million shades of doubt, its fine-grained mingling of virtue and sin. Do not be frozen by despair. Do not, as I did, wait to tell your tale upon a deathbed of regret. Regret is a profitless emotion. Fare forward. Take back your country and your soul. Start now.

The sun, I see, lingers. Amazing how long the days are, in early summer.